"This is _____

Edward Spellman anno____

Sabrina drew a trivia card for him and read: "An important ruling for witches happened in the year 1955. What was it?"

"Eisenhower was president," her dad mused, scratching his beard. "I say . . . that witches were allowed to play golf!"

Sabrina winced. "Sorry, Dad. Witches were allowed to trade in their brooms for vacuum cleaners in 1955. Even I know that. You have to draw a penalty card."

Muttering under his breath, Dad drew a Penalty card, and read aloud:

"Because of you, no one can have any fun.
All are banished to the Dark Woods,
Until you manage to roll a one."

The whirlpool in the center of the game began to swirl counterclockwise, and smoke filled the black pit. Their three tokens were sucked into the whirling maelstrom, and Sabrina, Salem, and Dad leaned forward to see what would happen next.

Suddenly there came a blinding flash, and huge tentacles reached out from the center of the board, grabbing all three of them. Sabrina screamed and Salem yowled as they were sucked into the swirling, magical pit.

Sabrina, the Teenage Witch™ books

Available from ARCHWAY Paperbacks

Sabrina The Teenage Witch™

Witchopoly

John Vornholt

Based on Characters Appearing in Archie Comics

**And based upon the television series
Sabrina, The Teenage Witch
Created for television by Nell Scovell
Developed for television by Jonathan Schmock**

AN ARCHWAY PAPERBACK
Published by POCKET BOOKS
New York London Toronto Sydney Tokyo Singapore

This book is a work of fiction. Names, characters, places and incidents are products of the author's imagination or are used fictitiously. Any resemblance to actual events or locales or persons living or dead is entirely coincidental.

AN ARCHWAY PAPERBACK *Original*

An Archway Paperback published by
POCKET BOOKS, a division of Simon & Schuster Inc.
1230 Avenue of the Americas, New York, NY 10020

ISBN: 0-671-02806-5

First Archway Paperback printing May 1999

10 9 8 7 6 5 4 3 2 1

AN ARCHWAY PAPERBACK and colophon are registered trademarks of Simon & Schuster Inc.

SABRINA THE TEENAGE WITCH and all related titles, logos and characters are trademarks of Archie Comics Publications, Inc.

Printed in the U.S.A.

IL: 4+

For Nancy, who loves games

Witchopoly

Chapter 1

☆

Sabrina levitated blissfully above her bed, looking like a sleeping ghost with sheets hanging off her head and body. Salem lay curled at the foot of her mattress, his snores matching hers in intensity.

Brzzzz-brrr-braat! blared the alarm clock on Sabrina's nightstand, waking her with a start. The teenager dropped onto the mattress and landed with a loud *sproing*. Yowling in fright, Salem leaped off the bed.

Sabrina looked up, dazed, her unruly blond hair spilling in her face. When the clock continued to sputter, she aimed her finger to silence it. Then she changed her mind and turned the clock off gently, feeling sorry for the poor thing. It wasn't easy being a teenager's alarm clock, especially when the teenager is a witch.

With a yawn, Sabrina sat up in bed, wondering what degradations of teenage life she would suffer today. Then she remembered something urgent:

It's the weekend!

So what am I doing up so early? Sabrina knew there was something she had to do today, because she remembered setting her alarm clock. *But what?*

Outside her window, the sweet chirping of robins and finches lulled her back into dreamy serenity. *It's almost summer,* she thought, as a gentle breeze wafted through the window. *Nothing ever happens in the middle of June.*

Sabrina's eyes drooped shut, and a peaceful smile played across her pretty face. *Whatever I have to do . . . it can wait.* In slow motion, like a falling tree, she toppled into her sea of pillows and comforters. Some adults thought they were good sleepers, but they couldn't beat a healthy teenager. Within a few seconds, sleep dragged her back under.

Sabrina heard vague voices, but she tuned them out—they weren't as real as the dream that was starting.

Since her life was so bizarre, Sabrina's dreams were often mundane. She dreamt of real horrors—like the cafeteria line, frog-dicing in biology, and pop quizzes in history. She didn't need to invent any freaky dream worlds, since those places were real—on the other side of the linen closet door.

The dream opened elegantly, with her walking into a big hotel lobby. A lot of well-dressed people were sitting around on sofas and chairs, while other people in white uniforms scurried past them, very busy.

Of course, thought Sabrina, *the people in white are the bellhops from the hotel, here to carry our bags!* She even had a suitcase in her hand, and she tried to give it to one of the white-suited workers as she rushed past. The woman rolled her eyes and pointed to the desk, where white-suited clerks were waiting to serve them.

"Of course," said Sabrina in a strangely deep voice.

Somebody tugged on her arm, and she turned to see an enormous woman waddling beside her.

"Stay calm, dear," said the woman, cutting a path through the crowd with her jutting stomach. "We're almost to *triage.*"

Triage? Sabrina looked around the dream hotel lobby. It didn't look as luxurious as it had before, and no one seemed too happy to be there. Wasn't a triage a place in a . . . *hospital?*

"Mr. Spellman," said a voice, slapping a clipboard into Sabrina's hands. "Please fill out the admittance papers for your wife—in triplicate."

"My *wife?*" gasped Sabrina. Planning to run away, she turned toward the gift shop and caught sight of herself in a mirror. She was Sabrina— but with dark hair and a moustache! She grabbed her collar and felt a tie, then she looked over and saw her pregnant wife, cruising toward a wheelchair that was waiting for her.

"Oh, no!" With a groan, Sabrina closed her eyes and fainted in the middle of the waiting room.

"Congratulations, Mr. Spellman, you're a father!" A nurse who looked just like Aunt Hilda leaned over her, holding a squirming white bundle.

Sabrina sat up and realized with a start that she was lying in a hospital bed. There was another bed in the cramped hospital room, but it was empty. Sabrina was embarrassed to be the only one lying in bed, when she hadn't done anything but pass out.

"I'm sorry I fainted," she muttered.

"Oh, that's all right," answered Nurse Hilda. "Lots of fathers faint, but they usually wait until they get into the delivery room."

"Or they faint when they get the bill," replied another voice. Sabrina turned to see Aunt Zelda standing in the doorway. She was dressed in a white coat like a doctor, with a stethoscope draped around her neck.

4

"I don't know how I became a father," said Sabrina with a nervous laugh. "I'm not even a man! I mean, not usually." She remembered the time when she had used magic to turn herself into a guy to try to understand guys. She had finally decided that she was quite happy to be a girl.

"It's not easy to be a father," answered Zelda, sounding like a wise old doctor from some soap opera. "Sometimes they get shunted aside, forgotten about. Everyone thinks only about the mother and child."

"That's ridiculous," said Sabrina. "Now give that baby to its mother, so I can leave."

"I can't," answered Hilda. "Since she knew you were here, she left to go shopping for diapers."

"Diapers?" Sabrina looked suspiciously at her aunts. "Hey, what exactly are you two doing in the middle of *my* dream?"

"Don't change the subject," insisted Hilda. "What were we talking about? *Fathers!* Does that ring a bell?"

Sabrina frowned thoughtfully. "Am I having this dream because I resent my father not living with me?"

"Maybe," answered Zelda. "Lots of fathers don't live with their kids, but they still love them. They still worry about their kids and do

5

all they can to keep them safe and happy. That's why we have a special *day* just for fathers."

Both Zelda and Hilda stared at Sabrina as if she were really dense. "Fathers," prodded Zelda.

"Day," answered Hilda, pointing to the baby.

"Oh, my gosh!" exclaimed Sabrina, bolting upright. "That's why I wanted to get up early. Today is Father's Day!"

"And you don't have a gift yet," added Zelda.

"Come on down to breakfast," said Hilda with relief. "We'll figure it out."

Poof! The dream abruptly ended, leaving Sabrina sitting up in her own bed. A big black cat lay curled at the foot of her mattress, swishing his tail back and forth.

"Oh, darn," drawled Salem, "you're awake. I was hoping I would get to play the *baby* in your dream."

"I can't get any privacy . . . even in my dreams," snapped Sabrina. She grabbed her pillow and tossed it at Salem, but the agile cat dashed off the bed before it hit him.

Ten minutes later, Sabrina was dressed and mostly awake when she appeared in the kitchen. Both Hilda and Zelda were dressed in summer dresses. Hilda wore a floral dress with a white Peter Pan collar, and the more elegant Zelda had a sailor collar on her chiffon dress. They looked as if they were going to an old-fashioned garden party.

While Zelda worked on her laptop computer, Hilda applied icing to a tray of warm cinnamon rolls, which smelled delicious. "These are for you," she told Sabrina.

"What's the idea of barging into my dreams?" demanded the teen. "Are you two practicing to be Freddy Krueger?"

"We tried to wake you the normal way," answered Hilda, "but your brain was not responding. So we took the sneaky way in."

"Sorry we had to rush you," said Zelda, "but we have to leave in a few minutes for the Goblins' Summer Brunch. So what are you going to get your dad for Father's Day?"

Sabrina edged toward the cinnamon rolls and stuck her finger into the white frosting. She quickly licked it off. "I, uh . . . I haven't decided yet."

"You always wait until the last minute," accused Zelda.

Sabrina sighed and shook her head. "What do you get a warlock who has everything?"

"I admit," said Hilda, "buying a present for our charming brother is never easy." She snapped her fingers. "He likes cuff links!"

"And how many pairs of cuff links does Edward have?" asked Zelda. "A hundred? A thousand?"

Hilda pouted. "Well, he always likes the ones *I* get him."

"I want to get him something really *special,*" said Sabrina, "so I can deliver it in person."

"He'll love anything you get him," Zelda assured her. "What about a black cape for the opera?"

"He has more capes than Dracula," said Hilda.

Zelda jumped to her feet and checked her watch. "If we don't go, we're going to be late for our brunch. And you know how angry those goblins get if you miss the appetizers."

"What am I going to get my dad?" whined Sabrina.

Hilda opened a drawer and pulled out a glossy catalog. "Here's the *Winsome Witch Catalog.* It's supposed to have everything for the sophisticated witch on your gift list."

She opened her hand, and the magazine fluttered magically across the room into Sabrina's hands. On the cover was a handsome warlock wearing a tuxedo and a red cape. Her father's style was more L.L. Bean than *Phantom of the Opera,* but it was a start.

"We have to go," said Zelda. "Don't worry too much about the gift, Sabrina. The important thing is that you remembered your dad on Father's Day."

"With a little help from us," added Hilda.

In their elegant party dresses, Hilda and Zelda swept up the stairs, and Sabrina chased after them. "I'll just look for him in the book!" she called after them.

"Good idea!" chirped Hilda. "Ta-ta!"

Sabrina watched glumly as her aunts climbed the staircase and disappeared into the linen closet. Light flashed from the cracks around the door.

Father's Day wasn't turning out the way it was supposed to—not at all. A girl was supposed to have a father who hung around and annoyed her all the time. But her father was a warlock, who was listed in a magical book and flitted all around the universe. He could go anywhere, do anything, and have anything he wanted.

How could *she* compete with *that?*

Sabrina tried not to be angry with him for sending her to live with her aunts. When she thought logically about it, she knew that living with two witches was the best way to learn how to be a witch. But it still hurt sometimes to know that her parents were split up, and she wasn't with either one of them.

She started leafing through the *Winsome Witch Catalog*. But everything looked so fancy, like monogrammed invisible handkerchiefs and magical polo mallets. *Is this the kind of stuff guys like?* she wondered.

Where's Salem? He's a guy. Or at least . . . he used to be a guy.

"Salem!" she called.

The black cat padded slowly into the kitchen. "Did I hear the can opener?"

"No, but I really need your help," answered the teenage witch. "What am I going to get my dad for Father's Day? What do guys like?"

Sabrina tossed the catalog onto the kitchen counter, and the cat jumped up to look. He casually pawed through the glossy pages.

"Ooh, here's something that's really *nice*," crooned Salem. "A magical scratching post for your familiar!"

"Stop looking for gifts for yourself. Think Edward Spellman."

"Wouldn't he like an engraved flea collar?" asked Salem, peering at a photo of a Siamese cat. "I don't think he has one."

"You're no help," muttered Sabrina. She leaned over the catalog and flipped the pages. "Family crests, condos in other dimensions. Is this really the kind of stuff he would like?"

"Maybe," answered Salem, "if he didn't already have them."

"Yeah, this catalog is worthless." She started to snatch the publication off the counter, but Salem pounced on it. "Hey, what are you doing?" demanded Sabrina.

"I noticed something," answered the cat. "These Winsome Witch people have a showroom in the Other Realm, in the Mall Dimension. It says they have a lot of items in stock that aren't in the catalog. Why don't we go there and look around?"

"Okay, it's worth a try," said Sabrina with a wisp of hope in her voice. She glanced at her yellow jeans and T-shirt. "How fancy is this place? Should I change my clothes?"

"Don't worry, you're with me." Salem leaped off the counter, dashed into the foyer, and led the way up the stairs.

A moment later, the witch and her familiar entered the magical closet. The door shut behind them, and an unearthly glow shot between the cracks as they entered the Other Realm.

Chapter 2

Sabrina loved shopping, so it was hard to ignore all the fantastic shops in the Other Realm and head straight for the Winsome Witch showroom. She and Salem raced through a whirl of colorful clothes, a cacophony of bizarre music, and the rich smells of perfume and exotic food.

Finally they entered the showroom through a small broom closet. The place was spectacular—like a grand ballroom—with rows of crystal display cases and miles of shelves. The shelves seemed to stretch forever into the shadowy distance of the showroom, and Sabrina had a feeling they really *did* have everything.

She looked into the closest display case and

saw glistening gems and jewelry from every realm and universe. Gazing into the distance, she saw that the shelves were full of magical knickknacks, books, sporting equipment, and antique clothing from historical eras.

Salem bounded over to the scratching posts, but Sabrina stood inside the door, unsure where to look first. That decision was made for her by an explosion of sparks and smoke behind a display case. From the smoke stepped a really cute guy with long brown hair. He looked hardly older than Sabrina, and he was dressed in jeans and a T-shirt.

"Hello! May I help you?" he asked cheerfully.

"Uh, sure." Sabrina stepped forward, wringing her hands. "Do you work here?"

The cute guy smiled. "Yeah, I do. To tell you the truth, I'm working off a debt. This store usually takes things in trade for the merchandise, and I wanted something special."

"Me, too, I want something special!" Sabrina held out her hand. "Hi, I'm Sabrina."

"Byron Conniver," he answered, taking her hand. His touch was warm, and Sabrina pulled her hand away reluctantly. Always at a time like this, the image of her boyfriend, Harvey Kinkle, appeared in her mind. Yes, she shouldn't be flirting, but Byron was a warlock. She didn't meet very many cute warlocks her own age.

Behind her, Salem cleared his voice. "Excuse me, but the catnip pouches are this way."

"No, no, Salem," answered Sabrina, forcing a smile. She didn't want Byron to see her lose her temper. "We're looking for something for my dad, remember? For Father's Day."

"Isn't Familiar's Day coming up?" the cat asked hopefully.

"We've got a lot of cool stuff." Byron motioned around the vast showroom. "And we're having a summer sale. All magical items are thirty percent off, and magical nose rings are *forty* percent off. They really flopped this year."

"I can't see him in a nose ring," said Sabrina, peering into the display cases. "He's got a lot of magical items. And a lot of jewelry, a lot of clothing, a lot of sports equipment. Let's face it, he's got a lot of *everything*. I mean, what do you get for a sophisticated warlock who's hundreds of years old?"

Byron smiled. "I bet having a daughter like you is worth more than all the stuff he has."

"Well, aren't you sweet," replied Sabrina, leaning over the display case and fixing her blue eyes on Byron. *You're not shopping for yourself,* her inner voice warned her. *Leave the salesclerk alone.*

"Okay, it's not likely I can get him something he doesn't already have." She tapped her chin thoughtfully. "Can I at least get him something *fun?*"

"Yeah, fun we've got." Byron pointed toward a distant section of the showroom, where stacks of toys and games were on display. "We've got a lot of neat board games. My favorite is Witchopoly."

"Witchopoly?"

"Yeah, it's a game where you throw dice, draw cards, and move around a board. There are trivia questions about being a witch and stuff. The neat thing is that you go to a lot of magical places, and the scenes are played out in the center of the board, like a video game."

"Wow, that does sound neat," agreed Sabrina. "I could play it with my dad, and that would give me another reason to go visit him."

"You don't get along with your dad?" asked Byron hesitantly.

"Sure, I do," she answered quickly. "But for the last few years, I've lived with my two aunts. At first, I thought it was because both of my parents traveled all the time. Then I thought it was because they were getting a divorce. Now I know, it's really because I have to learn to be a witch, which isn't easy."

"Don't I know," said the young warlock, rolling his eyes. "What about your Quizmaster?"

"And Boot Camp!"

Salem suddenly coughed up a hair ball. "It's

touching to hear all this nostalgia, but Father's Day is going to be over in a few hours. Can we get on with it, please?"

"Sure. Right this way." Waving his hand, Byron led them down a spooky, fog-shrouded aisle. As they walked along, the temperature grew colder, and Sabrina had the feeling that they were descending into a magical cave. That's why the shelves seemed to go on forever—they really did!

They finally reached a section of toys, games, and sporting goods. There was a whole row of magical bows and arrows, including the Cupid model. Sabrina heard a noise and looked up to see a toy train chugging along on an invisible track. A pogo stick bounced down the aisle all by itself.

Byron smiled sheepishly. "I let the toys get a little exercise. Don't tell my boss."

"No problem." She flashed him another flirty smile.

"It should be right here," declared Byron. He turned the corner and pointed at the top shelf . . . which was totally empty.

"Is this an invisible game?" asked Salem. "Or just a very small box?"

Byron frowned puzzledly. "Well, the games were right here. See—the card on the shelf says 'Witchopoly.' Maybe we're sold out."

"Sold out!" moaned Sabrina. "That's just my luck—I finally figure out what to get my dad, and it's sold out."

"We have other good games," said Byron with embarrassment. "There's one where you try to take over the world."

"Let's get that one!" enthused Salem, his tail swishing excitedly.

"Forget it." Her shoulders slumped, but Sabrina tried to muster a smile. "It's okay, Byron, I know it's not your fault that it's sold out. It's a popular game. I suppose Witchopoly is a magical game, too, so you just can't whip one up."

"I'm afraid not," answered the young warlock dejectedly. Then a smile crept over his youthful face. "You know, there might be some more Witchopoly games in the back room. It never hurts to look."

"Should we wait here?" asked Sabrina.

"No, you can come with me." Byron swirled his finger in the air, and a glittering cloud engulfed the two teens and the cat, whisking them into darkness.

They popped into a gray, grimy room with shelves rising to the ceiling. Every inch of shelf space was crammed with dusty boxes and goods, none of them looking magical. The walls were unpainted cement block, like somebody's basement.

As beautiful as the outer showroom was, this storeroom was ugly. However, Sabrina noticed that the shelves seemed to stretch forever into the darkness. This place was also huge . . . and magical.

"Ah, ha!" exclaimed Salem. "This must be where you keep the TV bargains, the stuff that's 'not sold in any store.'"

Byron shrugged. "I don't know why most of this stuff is even here. Maybe it's on lay away, or it was returned, or we're just overstocked. Let's look around."

Like an archeologist inspecting ancient ruins, Byron prowled the dimly lit aisles, looking for a game of Witchopoly. With a flip of his finger, he opened unmarked boxes and lifted dusty sheets to peer inside. Mostly they found old suits of armor, with broken and dented parts. Sabrina began to think that magical armor was going out of style among witches.

Byron stopped, closed his eyes, and concentrated. A tiny whirlwind of thought spun above his head, causing his longish hair to lift skyward. Suddenly his eyes popped open. He turned around and headed toward a drab shelf on the back wall. Sabrina and Salem hurried after him.

On the shelf were some old music boxes, ceramics, and a flat, cardboard box with blazing letters that spelled the word "Witchopoly."

"Bingo!" proclaimed Byron with a grin. "It looks like we've got one left." He reached down and took the game off the shelf. There was a thin layer of dust on the box, and it was slightly scuffed.

"Hmmm, I think this box has been opened," said Byron with concern. "Let me see if the pieces are all here." The young warlock opened the box and poked around inside, giving Sabrina a glimpse of the playing board and several of the ornate pieces.

"All of it seems to be here," he declared. "So Sabrina, do you want the last Witchopoly game? I'll give it to you for half-price."

Enchanted by the cheerful pictures on the box, Sabrina took the game from his hands. "You don't know why it's back here?"

Byron shrugged. "I don't really come back here much. The manager, Mr. Hawthorn, is the one who stocks the shelves out front. I don't see why there would be a problem."

"What is the price, if I may ask?" demanded Salem. "And remember, this is *used* merchandise."

Sabrina gazed at the box—with its bold pictures, bright letters, and promise of "Fun for Every Witch in the Family."

"Mr. Hawthorn is always looking for unusual goods," answered Byron. "A magical item, a beautiful antique, a spell, maybe even a good recipe. Since it's half-price, it doesn't have to be too spectacular."

"I didn't bring anything with me," complained Sabrina. "And I really need to take this with me . . . *today.*"

"I understand," said the young warlock with concern. "You can pay me later. In fact, it would be great if you could come back soon, when you weren't in such a big hurry. We could talk, hang out, and I could show you around. We've got a lot of cool clothes—and I bet you like to try on clothes."

"Give me a mirror and some clothes, and I can entertain myself for *days!"* agreed Sabrina. "Sorry, but I really do have to leave. So I can just take the gift?"

Byron frowned. "I'm supposed to get something for deposit."

"How about Salem?" she asked, only half-joking.

"Hey!" grumbled the cat. "It was *my* idea to come here. If it wasn't for me, your father would have another set of cuff links."

"I must have something to trade with me." Sabrina dug into the pockets of her jeans, but all she could find was a hair clip and four tokens for the video arcade. "Um, I seem to be a little broke."

"We'll take the tokens," said Byron, holding

out his hand. "I'll tell Mr. Hawthorn they're ancient coins of the realm—he's a little out-of-touch. You *are* coming back, aren't you?"

"Sure." Sabrina gave the cute warlock a smile, then dropped the tokens into his palm. She gazed approvingly at her box. "All I need is gift wrap and a card."

"Allow me." Byron took the Witchopoly box from her and tucked it under his arm. With a playful wink, he snapped his fingers, and all three of them were zapped back to the showroom.

"Watch." He stepped up to a wall full of crowded shelves, spun it around, and revealed dozens of spools of wrapping paper. They had every kind of paper imaginable, from cartoon characters to the most elegant gold-leaf and silver-embossed wrappings. Bright strands of ribbon hung from another rack, all set to complement the pretty packages.

"Wrapping is included," said Byron with pride. "Pick a paper."

As soon as Sabrina pointed to an ebony paper with crimson lightning bolts, a yard of the stuff curled off the spool, like a flattened snake. Byron held out the game, and the paper swirled around it. Within seconds, the Witchopoly game was perfectly wrapped.

"Yellow ribbon, I think," said Byron, snapping his fingers. A length of yellow ribbon snaked off the rack, curled around the package, and tied itself in a fancy bow.

Sabrina eagerly clutched the package. "This is just great, Byron. Thanks!"

"Don't forget the card." He snapped his fingers again, and an array of Father's Day cards appeared in the air, dancing. Each card flipped open and shut to reveal the sentiments inside.

Sabrina looked worriedly at her watch. "Gotta go!" Without looking, she snatched a card from the collection dancing in the air and stuffed it inside her package. "Thanks for everything, Byron. How do I get home?"

"The closet's right over there," answered the young warlock, pointing to a nondescript door in the corner. He looked a little worried. "I'm supposed to get your address, witch's license, and stuff like that, but I know you're in a hurry. You will come back to pay me, right, Sabrina?"

"You bet! Besides, I need those tokens back— I'm going for the high score on Gruesome Gore!" With a happy wave, Sabrina headed toward the closet door, which opened at her approach.

"Are you sure we don't need any angora litter boxes?" asked Salem, lagging behind.

"I'm sure. See you later, Byron!"

"Bye!" called the clerk wistfully, as the prettiest customer he'd seen in ages left his shop.

* * *

Sabrina admired herself in her bedroom mirror, thinking that she looked rather elegant and mature in her sleeveless, ankle-length party dress. She wanted to wear something cool, befitting the season, yet something dressy enough to go anywhere with her dad. Now that she knew her dad could go *anywhere*.

For years, Sabrina had believed her father was in the foreign service, roaming all over the world. True, he roamed all over, but far beyond the mundane world—to other dimensions, other realms.

He even had a girlfriend. It had been hard to forgive him for falling in love with someone other than her mom, but Sabrina had done it.

Father's Day was a good chance to relate to Dad one-on-one. She used to see him a lot when she was little—before the divorce—and she missed him. No matter what happened to the other people in their lives, the two of them would be father and daughter for hundreds of years to come. There was no sense holding a grudge.

Sabrina grabbed her present off the bed, then she opened a large, leather book entitled *The Discovery of Magic*. She thumbed through the book, looking for the dog-cared page that contained her dad's listing. The book was like a combination encyclopedia, directory, and yellow pages for all things magical.

When she found the small portrait of her dad, she placed the book on her bed and glanced down at her cat. "Okay, Salem, gotta go. Catch you later."

"Wait a minute," moaned the cat, sounding hurt. "You're just going to leave me here, all alone? Wasn't *I* the one who told you where to get the gift? Surely, you can take me along to see your dad, knowing how close I've always been to Edward. Besides, the game will be more fun if *three* play."

Sabrina sighed. "All right, but you have to promise *not* to be a sore loser . . . like you always are."

"The game is always rigged," muttered Salem darkly.

Sabrina turned back to the book lying open on her bed. Beside it lay the catalog from Winsome Witch. There were two ways to find her dad, she knew. First she could talk to his picture and find out where he was, which was like making a phone call. Or she could pop right into the book and surprise him wherever he was.

Sabrina liked the element of surprise.

Holding the gift-wrapped game in one hand, she reached down with the other hand and grabbed her cat. "Put your seatbelt on, here we go."

"Where are we going?" the cat demanded, suddenly sounding worried.

"Could be anywhere," answered Sabrina with a playful smile. "You know my dad."

With a bounce, Sabrina jumped high into the air and plunged feet-first into the book. With a sparkle and a jangle, the witch, the cat, and the game were gone.

The book snapped shut.

☆

Chapter 3

☆

As soon as Sabrina landed, she knew she was in trouble. First of all, there was no air to breathe, and there was no ground under her feet. Well, there was ground—but it was more like quicksand, shifting and tenuous. As she looked closer, she saw that she was surrounded by chunks of dirty ice. Above her was nothing but outer space, shot with countless stars, galaxies, and nebulas.

Nobody can see outer space that clearly, she decided, *unless they're in it!*

Sabrina nearly dropped the game and the cat, but she managed to hold onto both of them until she could cast a spell:

"Quick, on the double, give us a safety bubble!"

A huge soap bubble engulfed them, and Sabrina gasped for breath, surprised that she *could* breathe. She took a moment to look around and try to figure out where they were. They stood on a vast plain of ice chunks, which curved into the distance, where it was dwarfed by a massive yellow planet. The cloudy orb looked so close— and so huge—that Sabrina wanted to reach out and touch it.

With her A average in science, Sabrina knew this was a ringed planet, probably Saturn. And she was standing on the ring! But why was she here? And where was her dad?

"I want to go home," said Salem, shuddering in her arms.

With no sound and no warning, a fleet of sailing ships came streaming over the rise, hugging the ring of the planet like Windsurfers. The colorful vessels slashed through the ice on broad runners, which looked like skis, and their sails billowed in a magical wind. As they came closer, Sabrina could see a single pilot on each craft.

"This would really be a beautiful sight," said Salem, "if they weren't headed straight toward us! *Duck!*"

Sabrina ducked, but she was in no danger. The protective bubble was like a boulder in the middle of a racetrack. Several of the colorful sailing machines crashed into the bubble and went spinning off in all directions. Two of them plowed into the grimy ring and made large holes where they disappeared.

The rest of the sailing craft sped past her, with several pilots shaking their fists at her. "Sorry," muttered Sabrina with a cringe.

In amazement, Sabrina watched the ships that had crashed into her as they made incredible flips and graceful banks in the blackness of space. One by one, they glided back onto Saturn's ring and sped after the others, although they were now far behind. It was a beautiful sight, watching the colorful sails silhouetted against the bleak, yellow planet.

Suddenly a red ship with a silver sail veered away from the pack. It turned sharply, spewing a wave of ice in its wake, and headed toward her. Sabrina could see a bearded man in a silver jumpsuit at the helm. He leaned far to starboard to catch an edge, and the magical craft seemed to skim over the rings of Saturn.

The pilot looked quite dashing in his ring-surfer garb, and Sabrina could understand why women liked him.

The sailing craft skidded to a stop, spattering a wave of ice chunks against her bubble. Sabrina started to grin, but the angry glower on her father's face froze her in midsmile. He didn't look happy to see her.

"Sabrina!" barked Edward Spellman. "What are you doing here—in the middle of the Saturn 500? You disrupted the race!"

She waved her package at him. "Sorry, Dad, it's, uh . . . Father's Day."

The anger faded from his handsome face, to be replaced by guilt and confusion. "Did we make plans to get together today?"

"No, I thought I'd surprise you." She smiled weakly.

Now he looked annoyed again. "Well, you certainly did *that*. You could give a person some warning, you know."

"Your ring-surfer is really cool," said Sabrina, pointing to his craft. "How does it work?"

A smile crept across Dad's face. "Well, the sail collects magical energy radiating off Saturn's rings. Mine is a special design—it collects solar energy, too. We do this race every hundred years. I really thought I was going to win this century."

Sabrina frowned. "Sorry I messed up your race. I could, like . . . go away and come back some other time."

"No, no," said Edward, his expression softening. "It's Father's Day—I should have remembered. Shall we go back to my place and celebrate?"

"Sure!" answered Sabrina with relief.

"As quickly as possible," muttered Salem, screwing his eyes shut. "I'm getting vertigo."

Dad laughed and waved his hand. In his deepest, most bestial voice, he intoned:

"Sailing the rings of Saturn is fun,
But Father's Day has just begun.
It's time to vacate outer space,
And take the party to my place!"

He clapped his hands, and there was a bright explosion on the rings of Saturn. Four astronomers on Earth viewed it on their telescopes and thought it was an asteroid collision.

Sabrina found herself sitting on the porch of a luxurious villa high on a cliff, overlooking the ocean. The sea sparkled below them like diamonds spilled on a sheet of blue ice. Her long, summery dress looked perfect here, as she lounged in the warm sunshine and cool sea breeze.

"Chocolate milk shake?" asked her dad, seated across from her at the exquisite white-marble table. He picked up a pitcher and filled a tall glass with slurpy brown liquid.

"You know what I like," said Sabrina, gratefully taking the glass. She pointed her finger at the rim, and a straw appeared.

"Yes, I do," admitted Edward. "Knowing what a daughter likes is one of the prerequisites of being a dad. So how do you like my new villa?"

"It's gorgeous," said Sabrina, admiring the view. "Where are we?"

"Let me guess!" interrupted Salem, swishing his tail. "That's the Mediterranean Sea out there, and we're just outside Naples, Italy."

"Ah, very good," said Dad, clearly impressed. "Did you recognize it from the coastline or the architecture?"

"Neither," answered the cat. "I smell sardines and squid, fixed *ala Napoletano.* You humans don't know the joy of really being able to *smell.*"

"You smell all right," said Sabrina, "ever since you got into the garbage last night."

"I couldn't help it," complained the cat. "You threw away perfectly good chicken gizzards."

"Not to change the subject from chicken gizzards, but how's Gail?" asked Sabrina, referring pointedly to her dad's girlfriend.

He frowned. "She's off testifying before the Witches' Council. If it's not a legal case, it's politics. I swear, I never see her anymore."

Sabrina smiled wistfully. "How come you always pick women who work and travel all the time?"

"Ah," replied Dad, stroking his beard sagely,

"you don't pick love—it picks *you*. And how is your mother?"

"She's fine. I saw her last year when I took a spontaneous trip to Peru. Her new assistant is kind of cute."

"I hope she's happy," said Edward with a sigh. "It's hard for a witch to be married to a mortal—I didn't realize how hard."

He shrugged and shook his head. "Come to think of it, being married to another witch isn't all that easy. You get a little tired of each other, after a couple hundred years."

"Thanks for telling me what I've got to look forward to," muttered Sabrina.

"It was just a joke," said Dad. "And how is Harvey?"

"He's fine." Sabrina didn't want to talk about Harvey, because he was part of her normal life, a part she cherished. She always thought her life would be more or less normal, but that notion was dashed on her sixteenth birthday. Now she knew she was a witch, and the choice was to marry another witch or drive some poor mortal crazy.

"Happy Father's Day." She shoved her present across the table toward her dad.

"You shouldn't have." He grabbed the package, shook it, and listened to the rattling of game pieces. "What is it?"

"Why don't you open it and find out?"

"First the card." Dad lifted the card from the yellow ribbon and tore it open. On the front was a pretty view of a woodsy stream and two guys fishing. He read aloud:

"Dad, we dig worms half the night,
To catch fish by early light.
We scale them, gut them, and eat them,
And we hope we won't repeat them.
Your Loving Son."

He looked at her curiously. "Your loving son?"

Sabrina laughed. "Um, I was in sort of a hurry. But I spent a long time picking out the gift. Open it."

"All right." With a youthful grin, her father tore off the wrapping paper, and his eyes lit up when he saw the Witchopoly box. "Hey, that's great! I've heard about this game, but I've never played it. Do you know how to play?"

Suddenly a small scroll leapt from the box and landed in Dad's hands. He laughed with delight. "Okay, I guess it wants me to read the directions."

"I want to play, too," insisted Salem, bounding onto one of the patio chairs.

"Welcome to Witchopoly, the game that will

test your wits and your luck. Fun for every witch in the family!" proclaimed Dad, reading from the scroll.

"We'll be the judge of that," sniffed Salem.

Byron was dusting the display cases in the Winsome Witch showroom, trying to look busy. Actually he was thinking about the customer who had come in earlier. *Sabrina.* She didn't act like a witch—just a regular girl. And maybe that's what appealed to him about her. Most of the teenage witches he knew were stuck-up, full of themselves.

He sighed and made his feather-duster disappear. *She'll be back,* Byron assured himself.

The closet door opened, and he turned to see a small, bespectacled man carrying a briefcase. Mr. Hawthorn bustled into the showroom, straightening displays as he went. He was sort of bossy and fussy, but what boss wasn't?

Hawthorn hurried behind the counter, opened his briefcase, and carefully removed a ham sandwich. "The antique markets were brutal today," he complained. "Nothing decent—and everything at exorbitant prices. I might as well go to a swap meet at the drive-in."

"I made a couple of sales," said Byron proudly.

"Oh, really. What?" The manager took a bite of his sandwich.

"I sold one of the midpriced flying carpets," said Byron. "The J-1000. I got four season tickets for the Cleveland Indians."

"Excellent!"

"And I sold a game of Witchopoly."

Mr. Hawthorn squinted at him from behind his thick glasses. "Witchopoly? But we're out of stock. That game has been back-ordered for two weeks now."

Byron pointed toward the darkness in the rear of the showroom. "I got one from the back room."

The little man's face grew ashen, his jaw dropped, and ham sandwich fell out. "Y-Y-You . . . you didn't get one off that little shelf back there?"

"That little shelf under the pipes," answered Byron. "Did I do something wrong?"

"Did you do something wrong!" screeched Mr. Hawthorn, pulling his hair and giggling. "Yes, you did! The goods on that shelf are all *defective*. Their magic backfires! The Witchopoly game was the worst."

"But why keep them here?"

"I was saving them until the Bomb Squad could remove them!" Mr. Hawthorn closed his eyes and took several deep breaths. "I must remain calm. We're both witches—we can get the defective game back. How long ago was this?"

"Only half an hour."

"Good! What is the buyer's name and address?"

Byron gulped nervously. Now he knew he was in serious trouble . . . and so was Sabrina.

"I, uh, only know her first name. It's Sabrina."

"Well, you made a copy of her witch's license, didn't you?"

The young warlock grimaced. "She was in a hurry, and I, um . . . I didn't do any of the paperwork."

"What!" screamed Hawthorn. "This is preposterous! We sell a lethal product, and we don't even know the customer's *name*. Did she pay for it, or did you blithely ignore that rule, too?"

"She left a deposit!" Byron opened the cash register and searched the drawer. He took out a monkey's paw and a rabbit's foot, plus two glowing crystals, then he finally found the arcade tokens.

When he handed them to Mr. Hawthorn, the older man wheezed and sunk into a chair. "We're ruined! They'll probably sue us—if they live."

Worriedly, Byron asked, "What exactly does this game do to them?"

With a shudder, Hawthorn answered, "Everything that happens in the game *really* happens to the players."

Witchopoly

☆

Chapter 4

☆

The Witchopoly board lay open on a white
table, which graced a beautiful patio on a villa
overlooking the Mediterranean Sea. Sabrina, her
dad, and Salem sat studying the board, oblivious
to the crystal blue sea and the rumbling waves.

In the center of the Witchopoly board was a
black pit framed by a swirling whirlpool. According to the directions, it was here where
sights from the game were revealed. Around the
board was a serpentine path, with spaces clearly
marked. Most of the spaces had instructions that
had to be followed, and a very few had shortcut
bridges to other places on the path.

In each corner of the board was a deck of
cards—four decks in all. One was marked "Trivia," another "Luck," another "Reward," and the

last was marked "Penalty." The game was deceptively simple—the first one to circle the entire board and reach the "Closet" was the winner. But there were an amazing number of pitfalls along the way.

Their three tokens rested on the "Start" space: red for Sabrina, green for Dad, and blue for Salem. A six-sided die waited to be rolled.

"Let's roll the die to see who goes first," said Dad. He picked up the tiny cube and rolled a one. "Rats."

Sabrina grabbed the die and rolled a three. "Okay, I'm in the lead."

Salem picked up the die in his mouth and tossed his head, rolling a six. "Lady Luck is with me today!" crowed the cat.

"Now there's cat drool on the die," complained Sabrina, gingerly pushing it back toward Salem.

"Live with it," answered the cat. He picked up the die again, and rolled a five.

"I'll move for you." Sabrina picked up Salem's blue pawn and moved it five spaces, to a place marked Trivia.

"It looks like you get a Trivia question," she said, drawing a card. She read aloud: "Nostradamus was a witch. True or false?"

"False," answered Salem. "I knew Nostradamus, and he was just a lousy poet with a good press agent."

"Right!" exclaimed Sabrina. "Okay, here's your reward." She drew a Reward card and read: "If magical powers you lack, play this card to get them back."

"I'll save it until I need it," said Salem.

"My turn." Sabrina grabbed the die and rolled a four. She moved four spaces to a blank spot. "Dad, your turn."

Edward rolled a five and moved to the Trivia space. "Okay, ask me a question," he said confidently.

Sabrina drew a card and read: "In what year was Trent the Gent elected president of the Witches' Council?"

"Sheesh," muttered Edward. "That's a hard question. Was it 1374?"

"No, 1376. Sorry, Dad, you need to draw a Penalty card."

Her dad drew a Penalty card and frowned when he read it. "I lose all my magical powers."

"Too bad, Dad," said Sabrina with amusement. "Maybe Salem will let you use his card."

"No way," answered the cat. "My move." He picked up the die in his mouth and rolled it again. This time he landed on a Luck space.

Sabrina drew a Luck card for the cat. "Send the player of your choice back to Start."

"I send Edward," answered the cat. By itself, Dad's green token skittered across the board back to the Start space.

"I'm not doing very well," muttered Dad grumpily.

"My turn." Sabrina picked up the die and rolled a two. This put her on a space marked "Roll Again," which she did. To her chagrin, she was still two spaces behind Salem.

Dad picked up the die. "This is where I make my move." He rolled a five, which put him back on the Trivia space.

Sabrina drew a card for him and read: "An important ruling for witches happened in the year 1955. What was it?"

"Eisenhower was president," Dad thought aloud, scratching his beard. "I say that witches were allowed to play golf!"

Sabrina winced. "Sorry, Dad. Witches were allowed to trade in their brooms for vacuum cleaners in 1955. Even I knew that. You have to draw a Penalty card."

Muttering under his breath, Dad drew a penalty card and read aloud:

"Because of you, no one can have any fun.
All are banished to the Dark Woods,
Until you manage to roll a one."

The whirlpool in the center of the game began to swirl counterclockwise, and smoke filled the black pit. Their three tokens were sucked into the whirling maelstrom, and Sabrina, Salem, and

Dad leaned forward to see what would happen next.

Sabrina had heard of the Dark Woods, a spooky locale in the Other Realm, but she had never been there. She was looking forward to seeing this infamous place—safely—on the Witchopoly board.

Suddenly there came a blinding flash, and huge tentacles reached out from the center of the board, grabbing all three of them. Sabrina screamed and Salem yowled as they were sucked into the swirling, magical pit.

"Wow, this game is cooler than I thought!" exclaimed Sabrina as she sat up in a pile of damp leaves.

She gazed around at the aptly named Dark Woods. Giant, moss-covered tree trunks shot skyward, and the canopy of branches overhead was so dense that only a few feeble rays of sun trickled down to the forest floor. They wouldn't even have enough light to see, if it weren't for the Witchopoly board, which glowed softly.

Sabrina shivered from the cold and listened to the cawing of some very irritated birds. *If this is an illusion, it's an awfully good one.*

Her dad blinked in amazement at the towering forest. "I thought you only saw the scenes played out on the *board?*"

"Well, the board came with us," answered

Salem, circling the glowing Witchopoly set. Some of the artwork and place names had changed, and it looked as if the Dark Woods had taken over the whole Witchopoly board, including the cards.

"Shall we continue the game?" asked the black cat. "I believe *I* was winning, and it's *my* turn." Salem picked up the die and rolled again. This time he hit a three, and his pawn jumped out of the black pit and landed on the path—on another Luck space.

"Lucky," muttered Sabrina as she drew his card. She read the card to herself, then chuckled before she read it aloud:

"Your luck is not always so good.
You lose your powers in this foul wood."

"Oh, no, I don't," said Salem, nudging his card forward. "I get my powers back."

The cat's hair suddenly stood on end, and his whiskers stiffened, as if he had been electrocuted. After he started breathing again, he purred softly. "Oooh, that felt good . . . whatever it was."

There came a distant growl of thunder, and a soft rain began to drizzle on them. The sound of the rain spattering against the leaves was soothing, but Sabrina was still concerned about her pet.

"Are you all right, Salem?" she asked.

"Never felt better," claimed the cat, arching his back.

"Hey, I know we're all having fun," said her dad, shaking the water off his collar, "but isn't this game just a little too realistic?"

"Tell your dad not to be a sore loser," replied Salem snidely.

"Hey, I haven't lost yet!" snapped Dad, his competitive nature rising to the challenge. "No feline bag of fur is going to beat me at this game. Go ahead and roll, Sabrina."

"Yes, sir," she replied, grabbing the die. Sabrina rolled a four, which landed her pawn on a Trivia space.

Dad drew her card for her. He looked pleased, until he read the question and his face fell. "How come I never get an easy question like this? 'True or false? When making a potion, if you don't have any eye of newt, you can use purée of salamander.'"

Sabrina scratched her head. "This sounds more like a biology question than a magical question. But I say . . . true!"

Dad smiled and shook his head. "You can never substitute for eye of newt. Take a Penalty card."

Salem swished his tail expectantly. "Draw."

"Okay." Sabrina reached bravely for the stack of Penalty cards and drew the top one. After reading it, she scowled. "Your next spell back-fires, and you lose two turns. If you have no magic, go back to Start."

"I'm glad I didn't draw that," muttered Dad, "since I lost my magic." He glanced at the drenched boughs waving high overhead. "I wish this infernal rain would stop."

"Me, too," said Salem. Suddenly the rain stopped, and only a few trickles continued to fall from the leaves. After a few seconds, the trickles stopped, too. "Ah, that's better."

"My turn," said Dad, looking suspiciously at the quiet trees. He took the die and shook it vigorously in his fist. "Let me roll a *one*, so we can get out of here."

Edward hurled the die onto the board, and it came up two, which sent him to a Luck space. "Come on, I could use some good luck." He grabbed a card and began to read. A grim smile stretched across his handsome face as he read it for Sabrina and Salem:

"The player of your choice goes mad.
Every move he makes is bad.
An ugly monster he will be,
Until he somehow rolls a three."

Edward Spellman smiled cheerfully at the cat. "I choose you for this honor, Salem."

At once, there was a puff of smoke, a flash of light, and Salem disappeared.

With annoyance, Edward turned to his daughter. "Now was *that* supposed to happen? I don't understand this game."

Sabrina felt an insect buzz around her ear and get caught in her hair. She reached up to get it out, and her fingers hit something large and squirming. With a shriek, she jumped to her feet and brushed a four-inch-long dragonfly out of her hair. It looked like a model airplane as it flew off.

"Man, they grow them big out here!" she exclaimed.

"The effects in this game are impressive," said Dad, standing up and brushing the damp leaves off his silver jumpsuit. "I don't know what you paid for it, but you certainly got your money's worth."

"Yeah," agreed the teenager, glancing doubtfully at the foreboding forest. "You know, I'm ready to go back to the patio and my chocolate milk shake."

"Me, too," said Dad with relief. "We can leave as soon as we find Salem."

"Salem!" called Sabrina. "Here, kitty-kitty!"

"I'll get him back." Confidently, Dad snapped his fingers.

Sabrina looked down, expecting to see Salem at her feet, but the cat wasn't there. She scanned the dark forest, but the cat was nowhere in sight. It began to rain again, only much harder than before.

"Let *me* get him back," said Sabrina, lifting her finger.

"Wait a minute," cautioned her dad, looking around worriedly. "We read the directions for this game, and it didn't say anything about players *disappearing.* Maybe we weren't really supposed to come to the Dark Woods either."

"What do you mean?" asked Sabrina. "It's just a game."

"Is it?" Dad gazed down at the Witchopoly board, which was still glowing with a sickly green shimmer. "Let me try a simple experiment."

Edward held out his open palm and said,

"An apple a day should come my way."

He wiggled his fingers, but his hand remained empty. The warlock was in shock. "Oh, my gosh! I really *have* lost my magical powers!"

"Let's stay calm," said Sabrina, sounding anything but calm. "We can always find Salem later—with the book. The important thing is to get out of here." She pointed her finger at her dad.

"No, wait!" he called, but it was too late. Both of them suddenly disappeared with a loud *poof!*

Sabrina looked around, expecting to find herself back on the patio of Dad's villa. Instead, they were in an even darker part of the woods, and it was night. From the darkness around them came growls and skittering sounds. Eerie yellow eyes blinked at them and followed their movements.

"Hey!" exclaimed Sabrina nervously. "Where are we?"

Her dad put his arm protectively around her. "It's just a guess, but I'd say we're still in the Dark Woods. In fact, we're even *deeper* in the woods."

"But I tried to get us back to *your* place."

"Don't you remember—you drew a card that said your next spell would backfire. So we went the opposite way."

"Oh." The teenage witch looked down at the Witchopoly game and frowned. "You mean, everything that happens to us in the game is *really* happening to us?"

"It appears so," answered Dad.

"Well," vowed Sabrina, "I'm going to get my arcade tokens back from that store!"

A nasty snarl issued from the woods, and a pair of yellow eyes peered hungrily at them. They heard footsteps crunching through the underbrush, coming closer. "Um, Dad, what's out there?" asked Sabrina.

"Monsters," he whispered. "Griffins, sphinxes, harpies, bigfeet, stuff like that."

The growling grew louder, and more yellow eyes surrounded them, circling, moving closer. Sabrina could almost hear the drool dripping off their fangs. "What should we do?"

Dad took her hand, then he reached down and grabbed the Witchopoly board, cards, and die. "Since we can't use magic, there's only one thing to do."

"Yes?"

"Run!"

Hearts pounding, Sabrina and Edward Spellman dashed into the woods. They leapt over roots and ducked under tree limbs, just trying to put distance between themselves and the monsters. Sabrina dared not look behind her, but she could hear enraged growls, followed by large bodies crashing through the brush.

Chapter 5

☆

As she and her father ran for their lives, Sabrina stole a look behind her. It was dark, but she could see hulking, mis-shapen figures in close pursuit. The monsters squirmed, crawled, and leapt over each other, anxious to catch their unlucky prey.

One of the beasts had the bushy head of a lion and the scaly body of a dragon. Another had the beak of an eagle and the body of a goat. She didn't even want to think about that slimy thing with tentacles, or the hairy creature with wild eyes and long arms.

Sabrina tripped over a vine and fell down, and her dad dragged her to her feet. "Keep your eyes on the ground! Come on—let's go uphill."

She didn't even question this decision as she

followed her dad blindly into the thick under-brush. Sabrina told herself this was the all-city track meet, and she had to run like the wind. No, she had to run like a *hurricane!*

The brush slowed them down, but the hideous growls and crashing sounds made them leap like hurdlers. Something hairy made a lunge for Sabrina's leg and tripped her. With a scream, she tumbled into a patch of vines.

Her father whirled around and smashed the beast with his fist. The hairy thing fell back-wards, crashing into his fellow monsters, and it was bedlam for a few seconds. Sabrina scram-bled to her feet and ran ahead of her father. She didn't know where she was going—she was just running!

She looked back to see her father stumbling after her, and she gasped with relief. Dad's bravery had won them a few seconds' lead, but she still didn't know how they were going to get away from this pack of slobbery monsters.

Her foot struck rock, and she turned away from the steep surface. But her Dad grabbed her arm. "Keep going uphill—to the rocks!"

Now she understood what they were doing—they were trying to get to high ground. The forest wasn't only trees and bushes; there were hills and outcroppings of rock. It was a long shot, but they had to reach some kind of safety.

They scrambled up a steep incline, and Sabrina marveled at her dad's energy and bravery. The punch he had delivered to that monster's snout had slowed their pursuers down. The monsters were still chasing them, but none were eager to be the first to catch them. They were content to keep the chase going—to tire them out and run them to the ground.

Her lungs were on fire, and her legs felt rubbery from the exertion, but her dad kept urging her on. "Keep climbing, Sabrina! Keep moving!"

It was still hard to see in the darkness, but she could feel the crevices with her hands and feet. While they were climbing, Sabrina tried not to look down. If she fell off the rock wall, it was hard to tell what would kill her first—the ground or the monsters.

A couple of times she slipped, and her dad was always there to catch her and help her get her footing on the craggy rocks. "You're doing fine," he assured her.

"This is all my fault!" wailed Sabrina.

"I know, but you're still doing fine."

The growling and gnashing of the monsters grew a bit fainter, as they fell behind. Sabrina had a feeling that some of them weren't such great climbers. She strained to see how far they had to climb before they reached level ground, but there was nothing ahead of them but rocks, shadows, and treetops.

"I wish I had a flashlight," muttered Edward. "But I think we're almost . . . somewhere."

"Really?" asked Sabrina, panting with breath. She forced herself to climb faster, breaking another fingernail in the process. Now she had broken all of her fingernails, plus ripped her dress and wrecked her shoes.

Dad moved swiftly ahead of her, and she saw his lean figure vanish over a dark ledge. A few pebbles rolled down on top of her.

"Dad!" she called, alarmed that she couldn't see him anymore.

"Right here, Pumpkin." He crawled over the ledge and lowered his hand down to her. She had never thought of her dad as being particularly strong, but his grip was like a crane as he hauled her upward.

Sabrina scrambled the last few feet and lay on the hard rock, panting for breath, just grateful to be alive. "Are they . . . are they following us?"

"I don't think so," answered Dad, peering over the edge into the gloomy darkness. Somehow he had held on to the Witchopoly game, and he set it gently on the ground. It still glowed with an eerie light, revealing that they were on a plateau, not a ledge. A narrow path led from the cliff into a stand of dark trees.

"Where are we now?" asked Sabrina.

"I don't know, but I don't feel much like

exploring." He collapsed beside her and closed his eyes.

"I'm sorry," muttered Sabrina. "I ruined Father's Day, I caused you to lose your powers, and I got us stuck in this weird place that's full of monsters."

"Don't forget disrupting the Saturn 500."

Sabrina sat up. "I've still got my powers. I know my last spell backfired, but couldn't I try another one?"

Dad shook his head. "We don't know. It could be that your magic works, but it will only work in the context of the game. We have to admit it, we're under the spell of this game, and it's a nasty one. I'm afraid that we have no choice but to keep playing."

"If this is happening to *us,* what must be happening to Salem?" asked Sabrina with alarm.

Dad winced. "I don't want to think about it. According to the card I played against him, he should be a crazy, bad, ugly monster."

"Until he rolls a three," added Sabrina.

"Meow," grumbled the monster in a deep, gravelly voice. Black fur covered his arms, legs, stomach—everything but his gnarled face. He stood about eight feet tall, judging by the smaller monsters which scurried around his feet, waiting to do his bidding.

I'm undoubtedly the biggest, baddest monster in the realm, he decided. *I think I will call myself "Salem."*

He wasn't exactly sure who he was—it was as if large parts of his memory had been wiped out. The good things were all gone, and he only remembered the bad things.

Until recently, he had been a servant to a bunch of witches, and he *hated* that! He hated all humans, witches, or mortals. *They think they're better than monsters,* he recalled with a sneer. *I should just enslave them all and take over the world!*

Yes, that was an excellent idea! Just thinking about it made the big monster feel much more confident and happy. Taking over the world was definitely his thing. *There's something else I have to remember.* Yes, yes . . . *magical powers.*

Witches had taken his magic away from him—he knew that for a fact. But the nice game, Witchopoly, had given him his magic back. Salem flicked a nasty claw, and a T-bone steak— grilled rare—appeared in front of him, floating. He opened his hideous mouth, which had six rows of dagger-like teeth, and chomped the steak in one bite.

He crunched the bones thoughtfully in his mouth as he ruminated on the problem of how to enslave humanity. A secret attack would be good, but there were people who knew about him—the father and daughter. They had to be captured and silenced. Also, they had the Witch-opoly game, and he had to get it back. As far as the black monster knew, the game was the source of his magical powers.

He looked around at the greasy cave in which he found himself. The floor was littered with bones and scaly creatures crawling all over each other to get close to him. They slithered delightfully between his furry black toes. Hulking in the shadows were other monsters, respectful but unsure. They might attack him any moment, but Salem wasn't worried.

He knew instinctively that they were mere monsters—he was the only magical monster among them. No matter how big and strong they were, he was their better. They would be his minions.

"Where am I?" he grumbled.

"Who asksss?" hissed a serpentine voice in the darkness. Salem could hear the rustle of wings.

"Salem, the baddest monster in these parts."

"We have our leadersss," hissed the voice.

"Oh, yeah? Trot them out here. Might as well see what they're made of right now."

Thunderous snorts and footsteps sounded in the narrow passageway leading to the cave. "Who summons me?" bellowed a blustery voice.

The reptiles at Salem's feet scurried into the darkness.

"I did," answered Salem, his barbed tail swishing impatiently. "I'm taking over this operation."

A bellicose roar shook the cavern, and even the bigger monsters ran for cover. In a blur of movement, a gigantic, white-haired yeti burst into the cavern. Salem could tell from the look in his red eyes that he wasn't used to seeing a monster bigger than himself. Still the big dude charged forward.

"I warn you," said Salem. "I've got magic."

The yeti stopped and snorted derisively. "Like a witch?"

"Exactly like a witch," answered Salem, only he wasn't sure how he knew that.

The yeti growled and flung a mighty fist at Salem. The black monster purred, "Not so fast."

The yeti froze in midair, his fist inches away from Salem's face. The look of horror on the yeti's blue lips and red eyes showed that he knew he had made a mistake. He tried to talk, but his lips were frozen, too.

"You are the leader we have been waiting for for sssso long," said the hissing voice. From the corner shuffled a hideous, winged creature with a leathery, human-like face.

"I know," answered Salem. "There's nothing

worse than a bunch of disorganized monsters. We've got to get you folks into a program, and I've got just the one—*enslave all the humans and take over their realm!"*

"Yeah! Yeah!" came roars of agreement. Several of the monsters high-fived.

Salem stepped away from the white yeti and snapped his claws. The yeti crashed into a pile of bones on the floor and rolled over, shaking his head. The beast looked up, with a dumb but happy look on his shaggy face. "What is your bidding, Master?"

"Your name?"

"Grunt."

Salem pointed to the leathery, winged creature. "Harpy, what is your name?"

"Sssnark."

"Grunt and Snark, you must find two human witches who are in the Dark Woods. Father and daughter, by the name of Sabrina and Edward Spellman. Beware of the daughter—she still has her powers, and she can be especially devious.

"They have a board game with them—Witchopoly—and it's very special. Whatever you do, let no harm befall that game! It must be returned to *me.*"

Snark lifted his leathery wings. "What should we do with the witches?"

"You find them, and I'll use my magic to set a

trap." Salem grinned, revealing a hundred gleaming teeth. "While you do that, I'll organize the monsters of the Other Realm to take over the world!"

He gave a deep, satisfied chuckle.

The young warlock, Byron, stepped out of the closet with a paper party hat cocked on his head. He held a noisemaker in one hand and a trumpet in the other; streamers and confetti hung from his clothes. Although he looked as if he had just been to a party, he didn't look very happy.

Mr. Hawthorn glared at him from behind the counter of the Winsome Witch store. "No luck, huh?"

"No," said Byron glumly. "She's not at the Perpetual Party, the Health Spa, or the Dude Ranch."

Mr. Hawthorn consulted his personal Witchopoly board, now spread out on the counter. "As soon as they start to play, they'll end up at one of the locations used in the game. They'll probably get stuck there." He started leafing through the Luck cards. "There are only a hundred more places to check."

"A hundred more!" echoed Byron with a groan. He slumped down on the floor and shook his head. "I'll never find them."

"Not if you sit around here," agreed Hawthorn, bustling toward him with half-a-dozen more cards. "Don't come back until you've checked out these places."

"Mr. Hawthorn—"

"Don't complain, Byron. You're the one who sold her a defective game and didn't get her witch's license . . . or even her name."

"Wait a minute," said the young warlock. "Maybe we're going about this the wrong way. Where are the tokens she left for deposit?"

"Right here." Hawthorn opened up the cash register and took out the four arcade tokens. "But I don't see how these will help you."

"Maybe they'll give me a clue to where she lives," answered Byron. He took the tokens and squinted closely at the small lettering. "Yes, it says here 'Pete's Fun Palace.'"

"And how many Pete's Fun Palaces are there?" scoffed Mr. Hawthorn.

"I don't know," answered Byron. He picked himself off the floor and headed for the closet door. "But I'm going to find out."

Lying on hard rock, with tiny gnats trying to make a nest in her nose, Sabrina didn't sleep soundly. When she heard some scraping sounds, she bolted upright, sure that the monsters were after them. But all she saw was her dad, sitting in the glow of the Witchopoly game, working on something.

She looked closer and saw that he was using a flat rock to scrape tiny branches off a long stick. "Hi, Sweetheart!" he said, trying to sound cheerful.

Sabrina looked around at the gloom, which wasn't lessened by being a few stories in the air. She had a feeling that the Dark Woods were always dark, no matter what time of day or year it was. Now it actually seemed to be night, which made the place even more foreboding.

"What are you doing?" she asked, rubbing her eyes.

With both hands, Dad held up his long stick. "Making a quarterstaff. It's a kind of low-tech weapon, plus walking stick."

Sabrina shivered. "Are we going to have to keep fighting those things?"

"No, we're definitely going to get out of here, the sooner the better. I don't think it would be smart to just wander around here at night, but we can keep playing the game." He unfolded the Witchopoly board and began to stack the cards.

The game glimmered temptingly, as if daring them to try their luck. But Sabrina had other ideas. "I want to see if my magic still works."

"I wouldn't," answered Dad. "While we're under this spell, there's no telling what would happen. The safest course would be to keep playing the game—and hope for a lucky break. It's your turn." He held out the die.

Sabrina took the cube and juggled it in her hand. "Okay, here goes." She rolled a four and moved her playing piece to a Trivia space.

Dad picked up a card. "It's multiple choice. Ready?" After Sabrina nodded, he read, "A Witch's Toadstool is: A, a magical seat cushion; B, a poisonous plant; or C, a garnish for watercress sandwiches."

Sabrina scrunched her face in thought. She had heard the term, but couldn't remember from where—Boot Camp or biology.

"A magical seat cushion," she answered hesitantly.

Dad frowned. "I've got to talk to my sisters—you obviously haven't eaten enough watercress sandwiches."

With a heavy sigh, he drew a card from the Penalty pile and read,

"In Dark Woods, there are no safe places.
Swarms of bugs chase you back three
spaces."

The buzzing began instantly, and Sabrina could feel a prickling on her neck and ears as dragonflies got entangled in her hair. Mosquitoes swarmed around her bare shoulders and arms, biting ferociously, and she leapt to her feet and tried to swat them off. The gnats continued their assault on her eyes and nose, almost gagging her.

"Aaakk!" screamed Sabrina, flailing her arms at the invisible enemy. It was impossible to see them in the darkness.

"Stay calm!" ordered her dad. "Remember, the cliff is just behind you—don't fall off!" With his wooden staff, he swung at the cloud of insects, but it was like fighting air.

"I can't stand it!" shrieked Sabrina. "They're in my clothes, my ears, my *eyes!*" She stumbled over the game and began to run blindly into the woods, waving her arms like a windmill.

"Sabrina!" called Edward in horror. *"Look out!"*

Chapter 6

Sabrina felt the ground crumbling under her feet, but she dared not open her eyes. As the ground disappeared, she felt herself falling . . . falling . . . into a pile of damp leaves at the bottom of a hole. Even flat on her back, she couldn't get relief from the onslaught of insects—they just kept attacking.

"Dad!" she screamed. "Help!"

"Hold on, Pumpkin! I'm coming!"

Sabrina heard a thud as he landed beside her, and she felt his strong arms lift her up. Now the insects were all over both of them, pricking, biting, and stinging for all their worth.

"Dad, just leave me here!" she groaned.

"No! I've got an idea!" With a superhuman effort, he climbed out of the hole, carrying his daughter. As the buzzing swarm engulfed them, he managed to carry her across the rocky ledge and set her down by the game.

Through the blur of bugs, she saw Dad move her token back three spaces on the Witchopoly board. "Now," he said, panting, *"you* have to move back three spaces."

"What do you mean?" She swatted futilely at the bugs.

"You're standing where you were when you rolled," he said. "Now take three steps backwards!"

"I'll fall off the edge!"

"No, you won't—I'll hold you." His hands gripped her arms and guided her toward the cliff they had climbed to escape from the monsters. Sabrina could barely see anything with the bugs in her face, but she forced herself to look at her feet—and count.

"One step. Two steps." Her feet dropped off the edge, and she screamed—but her dad held her arms.

"Three steps!" he shouted.

As she did, the insects disappeared. One large dragonfly took a while to get out of her hair, but it finally did, too. Dad lifted her up to the safety of the ledge, where she collapsed.

"It worked," she said in amazement. "But I've got more bites on me than Salem's catnip ball."

Dad dragged the Witchopoly board over. "We

have to keep playing. Remember, the game takes everything literally. The only way to save ourselves from danger is to do exactly as it says."

"But it's Salem's turn," replied Sabrina. "Can we keep playing without him?"

"We have to. Unfortunately, he'll be a monster until he rolls a three, and I don't know how we can make him roll a three if he's not here. But, according to my card, if I can roll a one, we can get out of these lousy woods."

Dad picked up the die and started to roll, but he was interrupted by the sound of large wings flapping overheard. Sabrina peered up into the gloom. "What's that?"

The only light was coming from the game board, and Dad quickly shut it, plunging them into darkness. "I don't know," he whispered.

They waited, as the winged creature seemed to circle and take forever to go away. "It's not a giant vulture, is it?" asked Sabrina. "Waiting for us to die?"

Dad patted her hand. "Don't worry, I'll protect you . . . somehow." He shook his big stick at the black sky, but that didn't really make either one of them feel any better.

"Listen," said Sabrina, "why don't we continue the game in the morning, when we have a little bit of light. I like to see what I'm falling into."

"That's assuming there *is* morning in this part of the Dark Woods," said Dad worriedly. "You sleep, and I'll stay on lookout."

She kissed him on his cheek. "I'm really sorry about the game, and messing up Father's Day."

"Hey, what would a holiday be without a weird gift?" He rubbed the top of her head like fathers always do. "Good night, Princess."

"Good night, Dad."

Byron, the teenage warlock, walked through the twentieth video arcade named Pete's Fun Palace that he had visited that afternoon. The flashing lights, booming space noises, and happy chatter should have lifted anyone's spirits, but not his. To him, it was just depressing to see this regular place, full of regular kids. A place like this had been one of Sabrina's hangouts; now, thanks to him, she might never see it again.

He had in his hand a photograph of Sabrina which he had conjured up from memory. It wasn't entirely accurate, but it was the best he could do. So far, nobody in the other Fun Palaces had recognized it, and he was about to give up. He could always go back to searching the Other Realm, but he knew that was even trickier than searching this one.

As before, he went to the Gruesome Gore arcade game, remembering that Sabrina had been saving her tokens for it. He saw a couple of guys his own age hanging out there. One was short and dark-haired, and the other was tall and sandy-haired. He was playing the fighting game.

"Come on, Harvey!" cried the short one. "My token is up there—let me have a turn!"

"Why don't you go win a stuffed animal?" asked Harvey, never taking his eyes off the animated figures who were grunting and groaning as they pummeled each other.

Byron decided not to bother him. Instead he stuck the photo into the other boy's face. "Excuse me, have you seen this girl?"

He laughed. "Sure, I see her all the time. Isn't that Sabrina?"

"Yes, yes!" echoed Byron happily.

"What about Sabrina?" asked Harvey, turning away from the video game. As he did, some leopard dude picked up his karate guy and tossed him to the ground with a loud crunching sound. "Oh, man! Now you made me *lose!*"

Byron persisted with the shorter boy. "What's her last name? And where can I find her?"

"Her name is—"

"Quiet," ordered Harvey, giving Byron a very unfriendly stare. "We don't know who this guy is, and why he's looking for Sabrina."

"I'm from—" Byron started to be honest and tell them he was from Winsome Witch, but then he remembered where he was. It was possible they didn't know Sabrina was a witch, or that witches even existed.

"Are you sure this is Sabrina?" he asked, handing the photo to Harvey.

"Go ahead, Timmy, you can play my game," answered the taller boy as he studied the photo. "It looks like Sabrina, although she's a lot prettier than this."

"I know," said Byron, getting another stare from the tall boy.

"I'm her *boyfriend*," said Harvey in no uncertain terms. "So who are *you?*"

Byron tried not to show his disappointment at this news. "I work in a store that she visited today. She came in to buy her dad a present for Father's Day, but, uh . . . there's been a recall on the present, and I have to get it back."

"A recall?" asked Harvey suspiciously. "What kind of present was it?"

"Listen, it's really complicated to go into. Before I met you guys, all I had was her name and this picture from the security camera. If you want to come with me to see her, that's fine with me. In fact, I'd appreciate it if you took me to her place."

Harvey frowned at this idea, because he probably couldn't think of a reason to say no. "Well, okay. But you'd better be telling the truth."

"I am," Byron assured him. "I really need to get that gift back."

From the cliff, Sabrina and her dad looked with awe at the golden dawn glimmering over the treetops. Below them was a primordial world, untouched by humans or civilization. Until the dawn hit their rocky perch, they had no idea that they were on a vast plateau that stretched far into the distance. How far it went was impossible to tell, because the plateau was covered with gnarled trees. Only the buds on the trees were the color green—the rest were black.

"This is a big place," said Sabrina with a nervous laugh.

"We'll get out," promised her dad. "Shall we play the game, or walk a bit?"

"Let's walk a bit," answered Sabrina. "I don't trust that game."

They found what looked like a footpath through the woods, and they set off at a cautious pace. Dad held the Witchopoly game firmly under his arm. Within a few seconds, they were in such deep shade that it was like night all over again.

Still Sabrina's spirits lifted as they walked. It felt good to be going somewhere—anywhere— even if it was deeper into the Dark Woods. There were birds to watch, although they were black and ugly and made shrill calls. The only animals they saw were tree rats, scurrying among the fronds and leaves.

This forest had no flowers, but there were some pretty red berries growing along the path. The sight of them made Sabrina realize that she was getting hungry, and she wondered how long they had been gone from the real world. This was a magical realm, so the fact that it was morning didn't mean it was morning back home. Being impractical witches, neither of them was wearing a watch.

Sabrina thought about the tray of cinnamon rolls she had left on the kitchen counter. She had barely tasted them. Her mouth watering, she glanced at the red berries along the path. When she reached out to touch one, her dad cautioned, "I wouldn't. They're probably poison."

"Yeah," she agreed, "but they look delicious."

"I'll fix you breakfast later," promised Dad.

As they walked, the dirt path began to broaden and run straight through the trees. Soon it turned into a sidewalk with neat stepping stones—the first sign that something civilized lived in this horrible place. Dad took the lead, holding his staff in front of him, and Sabrina didn't fight him for the honor.

She was ready, however, to cast a spell if they really got into a bind. Even though magic was dangerous and unpredictable here, it was better than another bug attack.

Soon the trees grew stunted and more gnarled, and the ground was squishy and damp. They stepped into a clearing and stopped dead in their tracks. Looming in front of them was an ancient castle, rising from the muddy swamp. The old stones of the castle were covered with vines and moss, and it looked as if it might crumble into the marsh at any moment.

"Is it deserted?" asked Sabrina.

"It looks like it," answered Edward. Suddenly an awful creaking sound rent the air, and a moss-covered drawbridge lowered from the aged stones. With a splash, it fell into the swamp and seemed to float on the brackish water.

Sabrina chuckled nervously. "Is that an invitation to go in?"

"It looks that way," answered her dad. "Maybe somebody in there can help us."

"Or eat us." Sabrina gulped.

"You hold the game," said Dad. After he gave her the Witchopoly board, he walked ahead with his staff leveled for action.

They walked cautiously over the drawbridge, and the rotting wood squished under their feet. Sabrina feared it would fall apart, plunging them into the scummy water, but the bridge held together long enough for them to reach the stone steps. Sabrina held her dad's arm to keep from slipping on the slimy moss.

"They need to take out a home-improvement loan," she said.

They walked into a long corridor, lit by flickering torches. This room didn't even seem to match the aged stones of the outer walls—it seemed newer, as if constructed just for them.

"We can go back to the game," whispered Dad. "It's my turn."

"Not yet," answered Sabrina with a shiver. "Do you think there's any chance I'll wake up and find myself *dreaming* all of this?"

"Maybe," said Dad with a sympathetic smile. "There's not much difference between dreams and life. Both of them are real, for as long as they last."

Sabrina nodded and kept walking. Suddenly a jangling, clacking sound came from behind them, and they whirled around to see the drawbridge swiftly rising. In another second, it would be closed, and they would be trapped inside this claustrophobic castle!

Sabrina fought down an impulse to run for the door and leap into the swamp. But they had entered of their own free will, and there was no reason to panic . . . yet.

A thud caused them both to whirl around and stare in the other direction. At the end of the long corridor, a small metal door opened, and from within came a flicker of light. It beckoned them, as if to say, *it's safe here.*

Could it be a linen closet? wondered Sabrina with a dash of hope. *A way to get home?*

Her dad moved cautiously forward, his stick ready. The corridor seemed to stretch forever, growing longer as they walked, and Sabrina had the awful feeling that they were headed deeper into trouble. She wanted to turn and run, but the drawbridge had disappeared into the gloom behind them. She had a feeling it wasn't even there anymore.

Somehow they finished the long walk and entered the room beyond. It wasn't a linen closet, not unless a linen closet could be as big as a gymnasium. Her father gasped and stood at attention, and Sabrina saw why.

Against the far wall was a huge red chair; in that chair sat a creature that looked like a white gorilla, only bigger and meaner. Sabrina shivered. This was a throne room, and they were in the presence of a king.

"It's a yeti," whispered her father. "You know, an abominable snowman."

"What's he doing here?" asked Sabrina.

"Why don't you ask me yourself?" said the creature politely. "Come forward, and kneel before me. I am King Grunt, ruler of this mountaintop. I don't get many visitors."

"I don't know why," answered Sabrina. "It's such a charming place."

Her father motioned her to go forward, and

they took a few more steps and stopped. Following her father's example, Sabrina knelt down before the monster king. While she was on her knees, she heard the faint sound of wings flapping high above her.

She looked up just in time to see a hideous creature swooping toward her. With gangly claws, the monster pounced on the Witchopoly game and tried to rip it from her hands. Sabrina hung on to the game as if it were a life preserver, even when the beast spit in her face. It smelled like week-old fish.

"Dad!" screamed Sabrina

Like a home-run hitter, her dad swung his staff and crunched the monster on the head. With a groan, the creature let go of the game and slumped to the floor. The throne room shuddered with thunderous footsteps, and Sabrina whirled around to see the yeti loping toward them. His blue lips curled back in a horrid snarl, revealing a maw of gaping teeth.

"Retreat!" yelled her dad.

Clutching the Witchopoly game to her chest, Sabrina dashed for the door. Her dad chugged along beside her, but it was clear that neither one of them could outrun the fearsome yeti.

They stumbled out the door into the corridor, but they were a long way from freedom. Even if they reached the drawbridge, they would be outside in the woods, where *more* monsters could be waiting for them. Sabrina didn't want to take a risk, but she didn't have much choice. As the grunting yeti got closer, she panted,

"We're tired of this ugly place—take us home with great haste!"

With a bang and a flash of light, they disappeared. The yeti skidded to a stop and pounded his mighty fists on the floor. His enraged roar echoed throughout the crumbling castle.

☆

Chapter 7

☆

Once again, Sabrina found herself sitting in a pile of damp leaves, surrounded by dark, towering trees. Beside her sat her father, looking dazed.

He glanced around at their dismal surroundings. "Normally I like it if you obey me, Sabrina, but I'll forgive you this time."

"I don't get it!" complained the teenage witch. "I wanted to go *home*. You know, to Hilda and Zelda's house."

Dad sighed and picked himself up off the ground. "Don't you see, the magic in the game overrules everything else. This is the first place in the Dark Woods that we came to, so it's 'home' as far as the game is concerned. We're never going to get out of here unless we keep playing, and the game takes us out."

Sabrina unfolded the Witchopoly board and set it on the ground. "Okay, it's your turn." A large black bird swooped over their heads, cawing angrily at them.

"Let's hurry," said Sabrina with a shiver.

Byron and Harvey stood on the porch of Sabrina's house, banging on her door. It was late afternoon, close to dinnertime, but nobody answered their fervent knocks. Byron kept pounding on the door, as if noise alone could bring Sabrina back.

"She's not home," said Harvey, growing impatient. "Nobody's home."

Byron sighed. "You said her last name is Spellman. I'll look her up in the book."

"What book?" Harvey stared quizzically at the long-haired warlock.

"Does she live here alone?" asked Byron, ignoring his question.

"No, she lives here with her two aunts." Harvey scowled at the stranger. "There's something really weird about you. I think maybe you'd just better go away, and leave Sabrina alone."

"I wouldn't want you to worry," answered Byron with a friendly smile. He wiggled his fingers in Harvey's face and said,

"I'm the warlock you never knew. Of meeting me, you have no clue."

"What the—" Harvey's face suddenly went blank, and he stared straight ahead.

Byron sighed and looked around to make sure that no one was watching them. He resisted the temptation to cast a spell that would make Harvey forget about Sabrina, too. That wouldn't be fair, he decided.

"Time to head back to work," said the warlock with a sigh. He snapped his fingers and reappeared in the luxurious showroom of the Winsome Witch.

"Well," said Mr. Hawthorn impatiently, "did you find her?"

"I found her house and her boyfriend, but not her," answered Byron glumly. "But I know her full name—Sabrina Spellman. If she's not listed in the book, her father must be."

Mr. Hawthorn's pinched face brightened considerably. "Let's look him up."

He reached under the counter, pulled out an ancient leather book, and blew off a layer of dust. Hawthorn opened the book and waggled his finger; the pages fluttered past as he looked for the "S" listings. Finally they reached the article on Edward. Byron glanced over his boss's shoulder and cringed. "Uh-oh!"

"Uh-oh, indeed," muttered Hawthorn.

There was a blank spot on the page where a listing for Spellman should have been. Like Sabrina, her dad was lost in a magical jumble.

"Get back out there and find that Witchopoly game!" ordered Hawthorn, pointing toward the closet. "Or we could all lose our witches' licenses!"

"What!" fumed Salem with a mighty roar. "You let them get *away?"*

Grunt and Snark stood before the fearsome monster, their knees shaking. The hulking yeti pointed a trembling finger at the wrinkled harpy. "It was all *his* fault! He tried to grab the game too soon!"

The harpy touched a lump on his bony skull. "You didn't tell ussss—the man is a mighty warrior! And the girl—she used *magic* to get away."

"Of course, she used magic. She's a *witch,* you nincompoop!" Salem put his claws on his hips and began to pace the floor of the grungy cave. Snakes and lizards scurried for cover from his crashing feet. "Good help is so hard to find."

"What are we going to do?" asked Grunt.

"We're going to capture them again." Salem turned toward his minions and scowled. "When the girl used magic to get away, what spell did she cast?"

"But, Master, we don't know any spells," said Grunt, groveling.

"The exact words! What were the *words* she used?"

Grunt frowned and scratched the white fur under his chin. "She said, 'We're tired of this ugly place. Take us home with great haste.'"

"Ah," said the hulking black monster. "They can't leave the Dark Woods, or else they would have gone before now. So where would they end up if they went 'home'?"

He snapped his claws, and his gruesome fangs twisted into a smile. "I know where."

"Shall we go back to get them?" asked Snark.

Salem scoffed. "No! You two have already failed. If a monster wants something done right, he's got to do it himself. I'll turn into a smaller creature—one which they consider harmless. Then I'll grab the game and take care of those meddling witches."

His evil laugh echoed in the bowels of the grimy cavern.

The game of Witchopoly wasn't going very well. Sabrina and her dad kept getting stuck in quicksand and going back three spaces. Stepping backward wasn't so bad, but wiping the quicksand out of their clothes and hair was getting to be a drag.

While they played, Dad gripped his staff and

looked worriedly at the dark treetops. The monsters hadn't found them again . . . not yet. Even though things looked bleak, Sabrina was pleased and grateful that her dad was so quick to defend them.

"You're pretty good with that stick," she said. "Where did you learn to fight like that?"

Edward shrugged modestly. "Even when you're a witch, the Middle Ages are a tough place to grow up. I learned to use a quarterstaff when I was training to be a knight."

"Like in shining armor?" asked Sabrina, impressed.

"Yeah. But I never earned my shining armor. I was always more of a lover than a fighter."

Sabrina gulped nervously. "Dad, what . . . what if we don't get out of here?"

He gave her a brave smile and patted her shoulder. "We'll get out of here, Pumpkin, I promise. We just have to keep playing this stupid game. It's your turn."

"Okay." With a worried sigh, Sabrina reached down and picked up the die. She tossed it and rolled a six, which landed her token on a Luck space. As she reached for the Luck card, she heard the bushes rustling behind her.

Both of them whirled around in fright, and Dad jumped to his feet, wielding his staff. "Who's there?" he demanded.

"Meow," came a weak reply.

A moment later, a bedraggled black cat stumbled out of the bushes and collapsed in front of them.

"Salem!" cried Sabrina with happiness. She rushed forward and hugged her pet, who shivered pathetically in her arms. "Oh, my poor baby! Are you all right?"

Edward lowered his staff, but he looked suspiciously at the dark forest which surrounded them. "Where did he come from?"

"Who cares?" asked Sabrina, angry at her dad for not being happier to see the poor familiar. "At least he's safe!"

"That's debatable," said Dad.

"Oh, it was horrible," moaned Salem. "I was locked in a dark room for hours on end . . . with no litter box."

"Oh, you poor dear," gushed Sabrina, stroking his sleek fur. "We're so glad to see you. Do you know that we're stuck in this awful place?"

"I hoped that you would still be here," said Salem in a trembling voice. "Can we go home now?"

"I'm afraid not," answered Edward. "There's something wrong with the game—everything that happens when we play it really does happen to us."

"How odd," agreed the black cat. He licked

his lips with a little pink tongue. "Does anybody have a tuna-fish sandwich on them?"

Sabrina frowned. It sounded like Salem, it looked like Salem, and it probably was Salem. Sabrina had quicksand and bugs in her hair, and her dress and shoes were ruined. Her dad had lost his magical powers, and all of them had been marooned in this nasty place. Salem was a little dirty, but he was basically unchanged.

She thought about the card her dad had played on him. He should have turned into a horrible monster . . . with magical powers. She peered closely at her furry familiar. There was a strange gleam in his yellow eyes.

"Uh, Salem, how did you get away?" she asked innocently.

"I tunneled my way out—like a mouse." The cat reached a paw for the Witchopoly game. "Is it my turn yet?"

"No, I was in the middle of *my* turn," answered Sabrina. She pushed the cat away and began to reach for her Luck card. Her hand got halfway to the deck when she heard a grumble— like a bear coughing up a hairball.

"Dad! Look out for Salem!" screamed Sabrina.

But it was too late! In a flash, the black cat shot up to a height of eight feet and expanded into a giant, hairy monster, rippling with muscles! As Sabrina struggled to get away, long furry arms wrapped around her and lifted her off the ground.

"Sabrina!" cried her dad. He smashed his staff over the monster's head, but it splintered like a toothpick.

"Ha-ha-ha!" laughed a deep voice, booming in her ear. Sabrina squirmed, trying to get away, but the Salem-monster gripped her tightly.

"You wimpy witches can't hurt me!" bragged the monster. "Now give me the Witchopoly game, or I'll turn you over to my friends."

Growling, snorting, and slobbering with delight, a horde of ugly monsters came slithering out of the woods. They quickly surrounded the two helpless witches.

"Dad!" shouted Sabrina. "Draw my card! Quick!"

Edward lunged for the Luck deck in the corner of the board and grabbed the top card.

"Stop him!" roared Salem.

As the other monsters tackled her dad and threw him to the ground, he managed to read the card out loud: "Go to the Disco Dimension and take someone with you!"

"I take *you*, Dad!" shouted Sabrina.

"No!" wailed Salem through clenched fangs.

But now he was too late. In a spark of light and a blast of smoke, Sabrina, her dad, and the Witchopoly game disappeared from the Dark Woods. Led by Salem, a dozen hideous monsters

howled their displeasure to the top of the swaying trees.

Flashing, colored lights blinded Sabrina, and
thumping disco music—heavy on the bass—
deafened her. She looked down at herself and
saw that she was wearing bright yellow bell-
bottom pants and a pink halter top. Her bare
midriff was showing, and she was wearing platform shoes with six-inch heels. She looked like a
reject from the Spice Girls.

Unable to get her footing in the towering heels,
Sabrina stumbled. A hand grabbed her arm, and
she looked over to see her dad—he was wearing
a white leisure suit, flowered shirt, gold chains,
and long hair. He looked like a reject from the
Village People.

"Who says disco is dead?" he asked with a
smile.

Sabrina laughed with relief and looked
around. "Are we alone?"

"Not exactly." Edward motioned to the frenzied dancers all around them, all of whom were
wearing wild clothes from the 1970s.

Above their heads spun a huge, mirrored ball,
which reflected swirling lights to every corner of
the ballroom. On a grainy movie screen played
psychedelic blobs that must have escaped from a
Lava lamp. The dance floor itself was nothing
but colored panels, which blinked on and off as

people stepped on them. The overload of music, people, and lights was already giving her a headache.

Sabrina had to shout over the pounding music. "Where's the Witchopoly game?"

Dad shrugged and looked down at the floor. There lay the Witchopoly board, with people dancing on it. The cards and game pieces were being kicked all over the place.

"Quick! Pick it up!" ordered Dad.

Sabrina didn't have to be told twice. She dropped to her knees and scrambled between the dancers' legs, trying to grab all the pieces and cards. One thing was certain—they didn't want to be stuck here, in *this* place. That would almost be worse than the Dark Woods.

"Excuse me," she said, colliding into a dancer's knee.

A thin blond boy in a yellow Nehru jacket looked down at her and said, "Not feeling well, Dearie?"

"No, I'm looking for something."

"Let me help." The stranger dropped to the floor and helped her gather the last of the scattered cards. "What is this—a new version of Twister?"

"No, it's . . . never mind." Suddenly her dad grabbed her arm and dragged her away from the blond dancer. There was no quiet place for them to go in the vast disco, so her dad dragged her underneath a metal platform. Above them danced a go-go girl in disco boots and a fringed bikini.

"Be careful who you talk to," cautioned Edward over the thumping music. "Salem's minions could be anywhere . . . could be anyone."

"Poor Salem," muttered Sabrina. "He's turned into a horrible monster, and it's all my fault."

"Hey, I'm the one who played the card on him," said her dad. "I'm just glad I didn't play it on *you.*"

"At least Salem *enjoys* being a horrible monster," replied Sabrina, trying to look on the bright side. "Do you think he'll come after us?"

"Yes, I do. He probably wants the Witchopoly board, so that he doesn't have to go back to being a cat. Remember, Salem wasn't all that nice when he was a warlock, and now he has his magical powers back."

"But he's still my little kitty!" insisted Sabrina, feeling torn inside. She should hate his guts, but she loved Salem no matter how snotty he could be.

Edward sighed. "He's no little kitty until he rolls a three, or we somehow end this crazy game. He knows exactly where we are. The question is, does he have enough control over his magical powers to come after us?"

"Wild, man! Dig that far-out freak!" shouted a

voice. Over the blaring disco music came gales of laughter and applause.

Sabrina and her dad turned toward the noise and saw a hairy, eight-foot-tall monster wearing a purple fedora hat and a shiny purple suit. It was Salem! The ungainly monster was dancing like a maniac, as a crowd of people gathered around him. They cheered and clapped his every dip and twirl.

"What is he doing?" asked Edward.

"I think it's the boogaloo."

"Head toward the door," ordered Dad. "Slowly, so as not to draw attention."

They had only taken a few steps when they realized that the big white yeti, Grunt, was guarding the main door. He was wearing a lime-green leisure suit about ten sizes too small, and white fur poked from the seams. He peered over the heads of the crowd, and she ducked.

In the smoke and flashing lights, Sabrina saw something dark flying overhead—it was Snark, the harpy. Maybe he hadn't spotted them yet.

"Start dancing!" she told her dad.

Keeping their heads down, father and daughter joined all the other frenzied dancers. Luckily, their disco clothes were different than the ones they had been wearing in thc Dark Woods, and the monsters didn't immediately spot them. Her dad did a good job of hiding the Witchopoly game under his jacket.

"Okay, so now we know he has enough magic to follow us and bring his friends," said Sabrina. She stumbled in her platform shoes, and Dad gripped her elbow to steady her. "What do we do now?"

"While Salem is amusing himself, we've got to find some quiet place to finish the game."

"A quiet place—in *here?*" Sabrina looked around doubtfully. "It would be easier to find a quiet place on the *Titanic.*"

Edward craned his neck and peered upward into the gloomy rafters of the thumping discotheque. "I think I see a light booth up there. Let's check it out."

Still dancing, they worked their way over to a metal staircase drilled into a brick wall. People were hanging out on the stairs, watching the action below on the floor. Sabrina and her dad darted from one group to another, using them for cover.

At the top of the stairs, they found a metal catwalk suspended from rails in the ceiling. The narrow walkway had to be at least four stories off the ground. The catwalk skirted a row of spotlights and projectors, which produced the ameoba blobs on the movie screen. At the far end was a ladder to a darkened, unused booth.

Her dad nodded to her, as if to say they were to keep going up—away from their pursuers. As they started across the catwalk, Sabrina heard a clicking sound. Suddenly a spotlight struck them with blinding intensity, and they froze like chipmunks, caught in a bicycle headlight.

Sabrina knew she had to run, but when she started left, the spotlight followed her. Her dad dashed the other way, then the spotlight jumped to him, pinning him against the spindly rails of the catwalk. Comically, when father and daughter saw each other moving apart, they ran and met in the middle. The spotlight bathed them in harsh light, caught for all to see.

"What's your hurry?" purred a familiar voice. Sabrina squinted into the light, but she had to turn away from the glare. Skulking figures were moving up the stairs, headed for their precarious perch on the catwalk. She heard them chuckling and slobbering in the shadows.

"Don't leave yet," said the Salem-monster. "It's *my* dance."

Chapter 8

Sabrina darted left, then right on the suspended catwalk, but all she could see were monsters—advancing up the stairs and from both ends of the walkway. She could hear their demented laughter and the scraping of their claws on the cold metal. When she gazed into the spotlight, she was temporarily blinded, which was just as well.

She bumped into her dad, and he shielded her eyes from the glare. When her vision cleared, she saw him plainly—he looked oddly dashing in his disco leisure-suit and long hair. "Just stay close to me," he whispered.

"I can cast a spell," offered Sabrina. From the corner of her eye, she saw the big yeti inching toward them across the catwalk. He stopped just outside the circle of light, ready to pounce.

"Don't use magic yet," answered Dad. "I want to try something."

"Better make it fast." Sabrina could see the encroaching beasts more clearly now. Sparkling lights from the mirrored ball played off their matted fur and gleaming scales.

"Hold this." Edward gave her the Witchopoly board, then he removed the garish gold chains from around his neck.

"Dad, even monsters aren't going to wear *that* jewelry. Let me cast a spell!"

"Keep it ready . . . in case." Dad turned to a fuse box right behind him. Lights, metal boxes, and electrical wires spanned the entire length of the catwalk, and its main purpose was to reach that equipment. Not far away was the light booth, where all the wires eventually went.

Dad used his back to try to hide what he was doing. When Sabrina saw him stick his gold chains inside the fuse box, she decided that he needed a diversion.

She stepped to the edge of the catwalk and held the Witchopoly game over the railing, as if she were going to drop it. The spotlight followed her every movement, zooming in on her.

"Stand back, or I drop it!" declared Sabrina. "Those clod-footed dancers will pulverize it in a second!"

An enraged roar thundered behind the spotlight, and Sabrina knew that she had gotten Salem's attention.

The yeti lunged at her with a brawny arm, and she jumped back. At that moment, a burst of sparks shot from the fuse box, and the spotlight bulb popped in her face. Blinded again, Sabrina stumbled to her knees. As she blinked her eyes, she realized that she wasn't blind—the entire discotheque had been plunged into darkness!

"Hey! What's the idea? Where's the music?" erupted voices in the stunned crowd. "Turn the lights back on!"

In the darkness, her dad grabbed her hand and pulled her to her feet. "Ever see Tarzan?"

"Tarzan?" she asked doubtfully.

Scuffling footsteps sounded on the catwalk, and Sabrina knew that the monsters were on the move.

Slivers of light came from a vent in the roof, and she was able to make out the silhouette of her dad. He held a clump of electrical cables in his hand, and he gave them a good yank, showing they were firmly attached to a hook on the ceiling.

"Hang on to my waist!"

"Okay," muttered Sabrina. Slowly she tucked the Witchopoly board under her arm. Claws skittered on the catwalk beside her, and a furry appendage touched her leg. She grabbed her dad's waist and shouted, "Let's go already!"

"Climb over the rail!"

The yeti made another lunge, and Sabrina ducked under a sweeping arm. She clambered over the guardrail, gripped her dad's waist, and waited for him to yell, "Now!"

He jumped off, hanging onto the wires, and she plunged after him. Sabrina tried not to scream as they flew like Zorro through the dark disco—she merely hung on for her life. They whooshed over the heads of the audience, causing many of them to gasp in awe.

"Coming through!" cried Dad.

Soon they sailed upward, reaching the end of their arc. When they began to swing back in the other direction, Dad called out, "Time to bail!"

Like a couple of mosh dancers hitting the pit, Sabrina and Edward dropped off the cable into the surging crowd. Luckily, bedlam and confusion reigned, and no one was hurt. Sabrina managed to roll off some dude's broad back and land on her feet.

She looked for her dad and found him sitting dazedly on the floor. Sabrina helped him up, before he got trampled. After catching his breath, he pointed into the distance, and she followed the silhouette of his arm. "The door."

Sabrina could see a splinter of light, as a far-off

door opened and let blue neon spill in from the street. She grabbed her befuddled dad and dragged him in that direction. "Come on!"

It was a good thing she was an expert at clearance sales at the mall. Sabrina plowed her way through the startled crowd, shoving with elbows, shoulders, and hips. She pulled her dad behind her, and he quickly fell into her rhythm.

They weren't the only ones trying to get to the door, of course. Luckily, Salem and his minions had been trapped on the upper levels when the lights went out. The bad news was: it wouldn't take the monsters long to get down.

The other disco patrons were laughing and talking, taking it all in stride. Most of them were witches, Sabrina reminded herself, here to play a role. They looked upon all this chaos as part of the entertainment. A few others were permanent denizens of the Disco Dimension—they also behaved as people would in a real disco. No one freaked and used their magic.

It's all very stylish, thought Sabrina, *except for the monsters. You can dress them up, but you still can't take them anywhere.*

Finally they reached the door and fell into a conga line that was wending its way out. *Cha-cha-cha,* thought Sabrina as she joined the hip-swinging chain. Dad gripped her belt, and they danced their way out the door.

The insanity of the discotheque gave way to a

neon street, where everyone seemed to be selling incense and peppermint. Grungy boutiques displayed tie-died T-shirts and macramé purses, along with black-light posters and Lava lamps. It was like seeing a museum exhibit in a bizarre amusement park.

Although Sabrina was quite willing to gawk at the sights, her dad was anxious to keep moving. He gripped her arm and tugged her down a flight of well-worn stairs. "We've got to get out of sight," he whispered as they reached a storefront tucked away in the basement.

We're not on vacation, Sabrina reminded herself. *Whatever happens to us in this place—while under the spell of the game—really happens to us. Maybe other people in the Disco Dimension can afford to pretend, but not us.*

A sign over the door of the store caught her eye, and she read: "Madame Lavant—Fortune-teller."

Sabrina hoped that they still had a fortune to tell about.

Hilda led the way out of the linen closet, with Zelda rushing right behind her. Both of them carried potted plants with pretty ribbons tied around them, although Hilda's plant kept snapping at her nose.

"I need a leash and a muzzle for this Venus flytrap," complained the feisty witch.

97

"Hey," answered Zelda, "just be happy we didn't win the Baby Goblin door prizes."

Hilda peered suspiciously at her carnivorous plant. "Okay, I suppose it can eat the leftovers in the refrigerator. Nobody else will."

Elegant Zelda set her potted begonia on a table in the hallway and peeked into Sabrina's bedroom. "Sabrina's not home yet, and it's getting dark. I hope she's having a good time."

"With her dad?" scoffed Hilda. "She's got to be having a *super* time. They're probably lounging around his new villa, enjoying the view." Keeping her snapping plant at arm's length, Hilda started down the stairs.

When she reached the foyer, she glanced out the frosted window and saw a forlorn figure standing on the front porch. Hilda waited for him to ring the doorbell, but he just stood there. "Now who could that be?"

"I'll get it," offered Zelda, whose hands were empty. She opened the door, startling the poor boy who was standing there. "Harvey?" asked Zelda. "What are you doing here?"

He shook his head puzzledly. "I don't know."

"Sabrina isn't home," added Hilda.

"I know that," said Harvey, as if it were the only thing he knew.

"Well, come in," offered Zelda. "But stay away from Hilda's plant."

The teenage boy stepped inside the door. Although he had been inside their house many times, he still looked utterly confused.

Hilda set her plant in the kitchen, then returned to their guest. "So why did you come here, Harvey, if you know Sabrina's not home?"

He shrugged and shook his head. "I don't know. I was in the arcade, blowing my allowance . . . and then, all of a sudden I was *here*. I remember knocking on the door, and nobody was home—but that's *all* I remember."

Hilda glanced curiously at Zelda. It sounded as if Harvey had been caught in a spell gone haywire. Since many of Sabrina's spells went haywire, she probably had something to do with it. But she had been with her father all day, hadn't she?

"Hilda gets that way, too," said Zelda. "You know, she walks into the kitchen, then can't remember why she went in there."

"Thanks," muttered Hilda. "You should think about going home, Harvey. It must be dinnertime."

"Dinnertime?" he asked, suddenly alert. He checked his watch and frowned. "Man, this is crazy—I lost over an hour! Maybe those video games really *do* warp your brain."

He started out the door. "Please tell Sabrina to call me when she gets back."

"Will do," promised Zelda. She shut the door behind him and looked worriedly at her sister. "Maybe we should give our dear brother a call."

"I'll get the book." Hilda wagged her finger, and the large leather book levitated off Sabrina's bed and floated down the stairs into Hilda's hands. When she opened the stiff pages to Edward's listing, her eyes widened with shock.

"What's the matter?" asked Zelda.

Hilda pointed to a blank spot on the ancient parchment. "It's gone! Edward's picture, address—everything! It's like he doesn't exist."

Zelda grabbed the book from her and frowned at the partial page. "Something is wrong, but let's try to stay calm. The last time we saw Sabrina, she was going to find a Father's Day present. I wonder where she went."

"Maybe Salem knows." Hilda put two fingers in her mouth and whistled loudly. When the cat didn't appear, she ran into the kitchen and turned on the electric can opener. Even that didn't bring the familiar running.

"He's gone, too," she concluded. "Let me send Sabrina a thought-gram." She scrunched her face, tying to communicate telepathically with Sabrina. It should have worked, but it didn't.

"No answer," concluded Hilda, "although she could be taking a nap, or watching TV."

"I don't like this," said Zelda, rushing up the

stairs. She led the charge into Sabrina's room, with Hilda right behind her.

"The catalog!" Zelda grabbed the *Winsome Witch Catalog* off Sabrina's bed and studied it for clues. "A couple of pages are marked with cat scratches, but that might not mean anything. I see these people have a showroom. Do you think they went there?"

"We have to start somewhere." Now Hilda led the charge into the linen closet, which glowed ominously at her approach. If some harm had befallen her niece and her brother, heads would roll!

"Look, do you want your fortunes told or not?" asked Madame Lavant. She eyed Sabrina and her dad with a steely blue eye. That wouldn't have been too disconcerting, except her other eye was brown; it regarded them lazily through a half-open lid.

"Why do you keep looking out that window?" she asked.

"Oh, no reason," Edward assured her. "Well, actually we're on the lookout for some friends of ours."

"I'm sure they'll want their fortunes told, too!" gushed Sabrina. She wished she had kept her mouth shut when Madame Lavant stared at her intently with her brown eye.

The fortune-teller looked too young for the job. She would almost be pretty, thought Sabrina, if she weren't dressed in cast-me-down rags. Of course, many of the stylish people of this time period looked like street urchins. Madame Lavant was probably way cool, but Sabrina was in no position to appreciate her.

Her shop, however, was properly weird and interesting. Jars of herbs, potions, and witch's ingredients graced one wall, and old tapestries and parchments hung on the other wall. A doorway to the rest of the apartment was hidden by strands of colored beads.

Sabrina and her dad sat at the only table in the room. A green candle glimmered in the center of the table, and a water lily floated in a blue ceramic bowl. A tiny fountain bubbled in one corner of the room, and more water lilies floated in its shimmering pool. Despite Madame Lavant's dour expression, her salon was tasteful and peaceful.

"As to your fortunes," she began, "shall I read the cards?"

"No cards!" blurted Sabrina.

Madame Lavant smiled, showing a large gold-capped tooth. "Then let me read the bumps on your heads."

Dad gingerly touched his head. "I've got more bumps than usual. To be honest with you, Madame Lavant, all we really want is a quiet place to finish our game. If you have another room . . . a closet, someplace we could go—"

For the first time, the bizarre woman studied the playing board tucked under Sabrina's arm. "Witchopoly? I *hate* that game."

"Me, too," agreed Sabrina. When the woman frowned puzzledly, she added, "But my dad and I are really competitive. We just have to see who wins."

"Why do you hate it?" asked Edward innocently.

"Because my brother always cheated."

Both Sabrina and her father sat forward. "There's a way to cheat?" they asked in unison.

"Oh, yes." The hippie fortune-teller smiled and blew out the green candle. "There's a way to cheat at Witchopoly."

Chapter 9

Five dollars to tell your fortune," said Madame Lavant. "Fifty dollars to tell you how to cheat at Witchopoly."

"But that's ridiculous!" protested Edward Spellman. "What makes you think it's worth that much?"

"I don't think it is," answered the hippie gypsy with two different colored eyes. "But apparently *you* do." She glanced out the window at a commotion in the street. A big black monster in a purple suit was hassling people in a poster store across the street.

Both Sabrina and Edward moved away from the window, an action which Madame Lavant couldn't help but notice. "Uh, could you close the blinds?" asked Edward.

The fortune-teller smiled. "Are those your friends out there?"

"Who needs friends?" asked Sabrina with a nervous laugh.

"I think you two desperately need a friend." Madame Lavant muttered something under her breath as she closed the blinds. Sabrina had a feeling it was a protection spell.

With the blinds closed, the room became comfortably darker, and Sabrina relaxed a little. She couldn't relax much, because the monsters could smash through the flimsy door and windows with no problem.

Dad took the Witchopoly board and opened it on the table. "I'll level with you—there's something wrong with this game."

"Yeah, it's boring," agreed Madame Lavant.

"No, it's worse than that. It's cursed, or something. Whenever something happens to you, it *really* happens to you."

Madame Lavant leaned forward and fixed him with the blue eye. "Please explain . . . in detail."

"Why, you people are incompetent!" bellowed Aunt Hilda, staring from Byron Conniver to Mr. Hawthorn. She made a grand gesture which took in the entire showroom of the Winsome Witch Company. "You sold them defective *magic*—I should have both of your witches' licenses!"

"Believe me," said Byron in obvious distress, "I'd give it to you if I thought it would get Sabrina back. It was an honest mistake—I was just trying to please her."

Hilda frowned at the youthful warlock, thinking that he was cute—and obviously smitten with Sabrina. She couldn't hold either of those facts against him, so she directed her wrath on the hapless manager.

"You have no excuse, Mr. Hawthorn! You left a lovesick teenager in charge, and you didn't tell him about your lazy filing system in the back room. I'll have you before Drell, the Witches' Council . . . and Judge Judy!"

"Go ahead, sue me and take this shop over. Please!" said the fussy manager. "Do you think it's a picnic running this place? It's a never-ending headache, dealing with witches and warlocks. You know, this is really all the fault of the Bomb Squad, because they didn't get here fast enough to disarm that game!"

Aunt Zelda tapped a longer fingernail against her chin. "Hilda, didn't you used to date a guy in the Bomb Squad?"

"Yes, but don't interrupt me with pleasant memories," answered the fuming witch. Hilda rolled up her sleeves—she wasn't done with Mr. Hawthorn yet.

"Berating him won't do any good," said her levelheaded sister. "We've got to band together to find them—and the game. There's four of us now, which increases the odds. We better have a plan of what to do with the game when we find it. That's where the Bomb Squad comes in."

Hawthorn's shoulders slumped in his tailored gray suit. "There's no way to keep this a secret, is there?"

"No," answered Zelda. She turned to her sister. "So what's his name?"

"Oh, you mean Billy Bruiser?" asked Hilda with a modest shrug. "Pure beefcake—bulging muscles but not much upstairs—we got along great! I'll find him, if he's still alive. You're right—we've got to get the Bomb Squad on this."

"Byron, let me see the cards from the game," said Zelda. "What realms have you visited?"

The young man sighed. "The Dude Ranch, the Permanent Party, lots of them—but they could be moving around, too. We've got to hurry!"

"I'll find the Bomb Squad," vowed Hilda, heading for the supply closet.

"How did your brother cheat at Witchopoly?" asked Edward eagerly.

"Fifty dollars." The fortune-teller held out her manicured hand. "In advance."

"You mean, after you've heard our story, you would still charge us for some advice?" asked Sabrina, aghast.

"I would," answered the fortune-teller. "My job is to sell information. If it's valuable, you'll pay more, and I'll know I've done a good job. In the disco era, fifty dollars was a lot of money."

"More than we've got," muttered Dad, searching his empty pockets. He glanced worriedly toward the shuttered window. "Listen, how about a little credit? We're good for it."

"I'm not sure of that," answered Madame Lavant. "You seem to be in a lot of trouble."

Sabrina shook her head angrily. "She just wants to get rid of us. Come on, Dad, we'll take our business elsewhere."

Sabrina jumped to her feet and took her dad's hand. He looked at her with pride and admiration. "I have a lot of faith in us."

"When you get the fifty dollars, come back," said the woman snidely.

Sabrina whispered to her father, "You know, I could use magic to get some money."

"Don't use it unless you have to," warned Edward. "It might backfire, or *they* might detect it."

Loud, angry voices sounded in the street just outside the door; they were followed by the crash of glass. Edward turned to the fortune-teller. "Is there a back way out of here?"

She scowled, making it clear that there was, but she didn't want them using it. Dad held out his palms, as if to ask, *do we have to beg?*

Their hostess motioned toward the colorful beads hanging in the doorway. "Through there, up the coal bin, and into the alley. The coal bin is clean."

Dad grabbed the game and ducked through the strands of beads, but Sabrina hung back. "You won't tell them about us, will you?"

"No. And with the token of fifty dollars, I promise to help you." Loud banging sounded on the door, and the fortune-teller pushed her through the beads. "Now get out of here!"

There was fear in both her brown and her blue eye.

Aunt Hilda stood trembling outside a monstrous thicket of thorns—a wall of thistles, burrs, and spines. The gnarly wall grew so high that it disappeared into the clouds, and not even a bird would venture into that morass of daggers.

Hilda wondered if her address book had led her to the wrong place. She was about to turn back, when she spotted a small sign hanging off a big thorn shaped like a fishhook. Cautiously, the witch approached the barbed brambles and peered at the sign. It read:

"This thicket condemned by order of the Witches' Council. No admittance. Please step back 100 miles. Thank you, the Bomb Squad."

"Who would want to be admitted in there?" mumbled Hilda. When she bent down and looked more closely, she found that a small tunnel had been hacked into the monstrous growth. A few boards had been put up to maintain the floor in the tunnel, but they had been punctured by dagger-like thorns. Whatever the Witches' Council thought, nobody was in charge of this place but the thornbushes.

"Billy!" she called. "Billy, are you in there?"

"Who's that?" came a faraway voice. "Ouch!"

"What happened?"

"I poked my head on a thorn, what do you think happened?" answered a peeved male voice. "Is that you, Hilda?"

"Yes, my dearest. Can you come down?"

"No, we're sort of busy right now, Sweetheart. Why don't you come up?"

Hilda scowled, thinking that she had no alternative but to head into that daunting thicket. She got down on her hands and knees but realized that no sane person was going to crawl into a tunnel lined with spines and thorns. There had to be another way to get in there.

She said aloud,

"Oh, my, oh, my, I spy a fly, Oh, my, oh, my, that fly is *I.*"

At once, she turned into a tiny housefly. In this smaller, more agile form, Hilda could fly straight into the gnarly thicket and avoid all the thorns and spikes. She noticed a few spiderwebs nestled among the vines, and she carefully avoided those, too.

Wending her way upward, Hilda could see strips of clothing, rope, and shredded equipment hanging off the barbs. She figured the Bomb Squad must be having a rough time; maybe they would appreciate seeing a friendly face.

Another cry of "Ouch!" alerted her that she was headed in the right direction. This was good, because Hilda's sense of direction was useless. Everywhere she looked there was nothing but thorns, vines, and prickly bushes. The tunnel was overgrown and all but impassable, so Hilda zagged upward to make her own way through the thicket.

She found them—a pathetic crew of six workers, swaddled in bandages and lotions. Two of them were clipping away at the monstrous hedge with shears, but they were barely making a dent. Two exhausted workers lay on hammocks hanging from the thorns, and the other two were trying to piece together a shredded map.

Hilda buzzed around, looking for a place to land and change back into her charming self—when a muscular man jumped up and swatted at her with the map. "Get away, you lousy fly!"

"Billy Bruiser!" she scolded, but it came out a tiny squeak.

Another man sat up and stared with feverish eyes. "I swear, I heard that bug *talk!*"

"In this place, I'm sure the bugs *do* talk," grumbled Billy. Since he was still looking for her with a rolled-up map, Hilda thought it would be a good time to reveal herself.

She tried to alight gently, but there was no place to land in the thicket. "Owww!" she cried as she materialized in the middle of a spiny cactus. As she squirmed, barbs snagged her party dress and poked her hair. "Billy! Get me out!" she screamed.

The big man stumbled to reach her and free her from the spines. "Oh, Hilda, I didn't think you would fly up here . . . as a fly."

"You expected me to *walk?* What's the matter

with you, Billy? This place is hopeless—what are you doing here?"

The handsome techie scowled and pointed at their tower of thorns. "Some troll got hold of an outlawed growth-spell and wanted to play 'Sleeping Beauty' with his girlfriend. Anyway, he zapped a rosebush in front of his house, and it turned into *this*. The Bomb Squad can't leave until we clean it up."

"How long will that take?" asked Hilda doubtfully.

"About two hundred years," muttered one of the others. "*If* we can get back on schedule."

"What about the other emergencies?" demanded Hilda. "There are other spells and magic gone crazy, you know! The Bomb Squad is needed in other places."

Billy shook his tousled red hair. "We're not taking any other jobs until we finish this one."

"But there's a serious problem at the Winsome Witch," insisted Hilda. "At least it used to be there—now we don't know *where* it is!" She flapped her arms with frustration.

"Sorry, lady," said another worker. "We're under direct orders from the Witches' Council. Come on, guys, let's see if we can clear ten more inches before nightfall."

Hilda squinted her eyes at the formidable thicket and rolled up her sleeves. "I'll clear this whole place before nightfall."

Billy jumped in front of her and waved his hands. "Hold on, Hilda, you can't just zap it with witchcraft. That's why they called the Bomb Squad—if you try to disarm magic the wrong way, it can blow up in your face."

"That's what I'm worried about!" insisted Hilda. "My niece, Sabrina, bought a defective game of Witchopoly, which the Bomb Squad was supposed to pick up." Waving her hands, Hilda told the whole story of the missing game, missing daughter, and missing father.

Billy rubbed his chin. "Oh, that *is* serious. That's what we call a mystical inverted transference multiplier. I'm not sure I can defuse it— our only hope may be to blow up the game."

"Blow up the game?" asked Hilda in horror.

"From a safe distance, of course," answered the specialist. "You see, if anybody assaults that game with magic, which your friends probably have already done, it will overload and explode. Of course, they might be playing the game fairly, trying to win, in which case it shouldn't overload. Weird, inverted magic will be happening to them, but they might survive that. Excuse me."

He pointed to one of the workers with the shears. "You know this stuff, Fred, so get back to work."

"Yeah, boss," answered the man with a wave.

Billy lowered his voice to say, "We have the same problem here. The magic is so overloaded in this darn rosebush that we have to cut it back the regular way."

"Can't you hire gardeners to do that?" demanded Hilda.

"And let everyone know we can't finish the job?" scoffed Billy. "I don't think so."

Hilda shook her head in frustration. *If they were mental giants, they wouldn't be on the Bomb Squad,* she told herself. She still needed their help.

"Missing a day's work in here won't set you back too much time," she said sweetly, "but it would be a big favor to me." She stroked his grimy cheek.

Billy gulped. "But if the Witches' Council ever found out—"

Hilda glanced around at the thistles, thorns, and weary workers. She forced a smile. "I know, you wouldn't want to lose this *great* job, but you won't have to. I'll keep the Witches' Council busy, and they'll never know anything about your helping us."

"How are you going to do that?" asked Billy.

"Don't worry about it," she answered pleasantly as she straightened his collar. "Just have your squad tidy up here, so that you'll be ready to go when I call you. Time is of the essence."

Billy cringed. "No kidding. I wouldn't want to be around that Witchopoly game when it blows."

"How can we find it?" asked Hilda, getting serious.

"Check *News of the Other Realm*. See if strange stuff has been happening anywhere else."

"Good idea. Catch you soon." Hilda snapped her fingers and was transported back to the Winsome Witch showroom. The only one present was Mr. Hawthorn, who was busy on the phone. When he saw her, he quickly hung up.

"Hello," he said with a nervous laugh. "I was just checking with some of my colleagues."

"You mean your lawyers, don't you?" Hilda scowled. "You're not in trouble yet, Hawthorn, but you could be—big time. I just found out from the Bomb Squad that the game you sold my niece could overload and explode!"

"Oh, dear! When is the Bomb Squad coming?"

"Not until we need them." Hilda strode to the counter, grabbed the leather-bound book, and opened it. "Where are Zelda and Byron?"

"Out looking. I'm keeping track of where they've been." Hawthorn pointed eagerly to his notepad and Witchopoly board. "What are you doing?"

"I need to recruit more help. Ah, here she is!"

Hilda pointed to a drawing of Edward's attractive girlfriend. "Hello, Gail! I need to talk to you."

When the drawing saw who it was, she turned away. "Not now, Hilda, I'm in the middle of something important. Can I call you back next week?"

"This is important, too!" insisted the older witch. "Edward is in a lot of trouble, and so is Sabrina."

The woman in the business suit whirled around, and her image became crisp and clear. So did the worry on her face. "What did they get into now?"

Hilda gave her a brief but harrowing version of events. "So, if we don't find them soon, something really bad could happen to them. Maybe it already has."

"What can I do?" asked Gail with concern.

"I need you to distract the Witches' Council, so that they won't know I stole the Bomb Squad."

Gail nodded forcefully. "Okay, I can do that. Goodness knows, they're not hard to distract. Anything else?"

"That's it for now. Keep in touch." Hilda shut the book and turned to Mr. Hawthorn. "In all this junk, you must have a magical 3-D viewer. Turn on *News of the Other Realm* and watch to see what's happening. If there's anything strange or inexplicable, that might be them. Can you do that?"

"Sure," answered Hawthorn. He stood on his tiptoes and peered into the vast depths of merchandise. "I've got one right back there."

"Move it!" bellowed Hilda. "My family is in trouble!"

☆

Chapter 10

☆

"Run!" said Sabrina, panting. "Hide under the cans!"

The teenage witch, dressed like a disco diva, ducked into a row of garbage cans that littered the alley. She rapped on them until she found an empty one, then she turned it upside down and crawled inside. Sabrina didn't cover herself with the can until she made sure her father was doing the same thing.

Dad looked disgusted at the idea of hiding in a dirty garbage can, but the shadow of that thing in the sky was coming closer.

Their nemesis, Salem, was using the harpy, the griffin, and other flying beasts as helicopters, searching for them from the sky. Twice they had collapsed into deserted corners, only to be chased out by monsters looking for them.

Luckily, the monsters made a lot of noise and caused a commotion wherever they went, or the Spellmans surely would have been caught by now. Still the beasts were not giving up their search. Sabrina had a feeling that Salem just wanted to make sure they had no time to sit and play the game.

Her dad wasn't hiding. "Come on!" she insisted.

Facing reality, he lifted the lid of a large Dumpster and vaulted inside. He only closed the lid partly, so that he could observe the alley . . . and the winged being which cruised overhead.

Sabrina lowered her garbage can and tried to keep from shivering in the darkness. Once again, she fought the temptation to cast a spell. She could have used magical light, vision through metal, a subway home, or any number of spells. True, magic had gotten them into this mess, and it had backfired every time she had tried it. Still, Sabrina knew she might have to try again.

But her dad was cautious. He had lost his own magical power to the Witchopoly game, and he was trying not to get burned again. That meant winning the game, although Sabrina had a feeling they weren't winning.

Knuckles rapped on her garbage can, startling

the girl. "Okay," said a weary voice. "It's gone. Come on out."

Sabrina tipped over the garbage can and crawled out. Both she and her father now looked like scruffy street people—bedraggled hippies, and proud of it. They smelled like old banana peels and coffee grounds. Sabrina shook her head and began to laugh.

"I don't know what's so funny," muttered Dad.

"Us. We started out elegant today, and now we're like total grunge." Sabrina covered her mouth, but she couldn't stop laughing.

"Yeah," answered Dad with a begrudging smile. "Maybe we needed a dose of humility. I know I'm a lot more humble than I was before. It's a drag not having magical powers—I'll never look down on mortals again."

"Now what?" asked Sabrina. "Keep playing?"

Dad looked around cautiously, then he pushed the Dumpster a few feet, making a small space between it and the wall. In this space, he set up the game board. Sabrina was impressed when he opened the lid of the Dumpster and propped it open to create a roof for their little hiding place. Even from the air, they were camouflaged.

"My move," said Dad, picking up the die. With a hopeful sigh, he rolled. "A two," he said absently. "Why can't I ever roll a *one?"*

"You landed on a Trivia space," Sabrina pointed out. Dad nodded to her, and she reached for a card. As she read the card, a smile played across her face. "You have a chance on this one, Dad. Survey says: What is the most popular animal for a witch's familiar?"

"I hate to be mundane," said Edward, "but is it a cat?"

"Bingo!" answered Sabrina with a grin. "You get to draw a Reward card."

With fingers wiggling nervously, Dad drew a card and read it. At first he smiled, then he looked troubled. "I can go to the Circus World, if I wish." He frowned and repeated, "If I wish."

Sabrina slapped her knees and grinned. "That's great! Go to the Circus World—get out of here while you can."

"But I don't want to leave *you.*"

"I still have my magical powers," said Sabrina, trying to sound brave. "You don't, so you're more at risk. If worse comes to worse, I'll just go there by magic. You know, I haven't been to the Circus World since you took me as a little kid."

"I remember that," answered Dad with a wistful smile. "You thought it was a regular circus, and I didn't tell you differently. We used to have lots of fun, didn't we, Pumpkin?"

She nodded. "We sure did. By the way, you gotta go."

"Who will take the game?" asked Dad.

The teenager shrugged. "I guess it stays with me, since it's my turn next. Go on, Dad. I'll be okay, really."

"No," he said decisively, shaking his head. "We're a team—we're in this together. I can't go without my little girl."

"I wish you would, but it's your choice." Feeling both relieved and annoyed at her dad's decision, Sabrina picked up the die. "Once I roll, you lose your chance."

"Go on," he answered with a smile. "We're traveling together."

Before Sabrina could roll the die, she heard a shuffling sound out in the alley. Both of them peered cautiously around the corner of the dumpster, trying to see as much as they could. Grunt, the big white yeti, came loping down the deserted byway. When he stopped to sniff the air, they quickly ducked behind cover.

Dad put his finger to his lips, but Sabrina wasn't going to say anything. She could barely breathe. If the yeti was sniffing the air for them, he obviously remembered what they smelled like. Of course, now they smelled mostly like garbage; Sabrina didn't know whether that was good or bad.

Finally they heard the yeti grunt and shuffle on, not having detected them. Nevertheless, her dad folded up the game and shook his head. "It's too dangerous here. We have to find somewhere else to go."

"What about Circus World?" asked Sabrina. *"You* could still go."

He leaned into the Dumpster and started rooting around in the garbage, causing Sabrina to scowl. "What are you looking for?"

"Something worth fifty dollars. I'm ready to return to that fortune-teller—and admit we need help. You'd be surprised what people would throw away, especially witches on vacation."

With a victorious grin, Edward pulled out a small black satchel, which looked like something a doctor would carry. "Hmmm. I think we should open it, don't you?"

"Go ahead." Sabrina tried to sound blasé, but she was curious, too.

With some difficulty, he pried the latch open and ended up spilling diamond and ruby jewelry into the garbage. At least, the pieces looked like diamonds and rubies, but they could be costume jewelry, thought Sabrina. The Dumpster hiding-place suggested that they weren't too valuable.

But the Disco Dimension was populated by witches and warlocks, to whom real gems were nothing but trinkets to be conjured at will.

Dad scowled as he picked up a tiara. "If I had my powers, I could tell you if these are real. But it's all we've got—let's see if Madame Lavant will take them."

"She's a witch, pretending to be a hippie," muttered Sabrina. "I don't even know why she needs fifty dollars."

"This is the Disco Dimension. If she rips us off for a fair sum, she'll feel as if she's playing her role to the max. Without using magic. It's the principle of the thing. You'll learn that, for witches, playing normal in a normal world is the hardest job of all."

Edward motioned around them. "That's why this weird dimension has been saved in pristine condition—to remind us that mortals aren't normal either."

With a wave, Dad led the way out of the alley into the street, where they blended in with a throng of disco revelers. They didn't hear the laughter behind them at the end of the dark alley.

Like two hairy salt- and pepper-shakers, a black monster and a white monster popped their heads from a dark stairwell. As they watched their prey disappear into the crowd, the black monster sniggered. "There they go. Right into our trap."

"How did you know they would take the bag of jewels?" asked the yeti.

Salem sneered, showing a row of jagged fangs.

125

"Mortal or witch, they always fall for a bag of jewels. Witches are also lazy. If you give them an easy way out, they'll take it. Come on, Grunt, I want to make sure everything is ready. I won't let them use their magic this time."

Snorting with satisfaction, the hulking black monster crawled from the stairwell and stretched to his full height of eight feet. *Gosh, it feels good to be bad!*

Still there was a slight pang of guilt somewhere deep in his mangy carcass. The monster wouldn't call it a serious burst of conscience, but it was enough to give him indigestion. He belched loudly and felt much better. Still the Salem-monster was troubled.

Why should I feel bad about defeating that sniveling witch and her bumbling father? What are they to me?

He couldn't figure it out. Salem knew that he didn't have a good side, so it couldn't be that. The fearsome monster roared in anger, and the giant yeti cowered in submission.

Mr. Hawthorn lowered the little toy view-scope, which was a plastic gizmo used to view 3-D photos. The manager of the Winsome Witch rubbed his eyes and said, "According to the news, there have been some disturbances in the Disco Dimension. Do you know that place?"

"No," said Aunt Zelda.

"Yes," answered Hilda.

The two sisters looked at one another, and Zelda smiled knowingly.

"Well, I've heard of it," said Hilda. "I happen to like Donna Summers, okay?"

"Me, too," answered Zelda. "So who's going to check it out? I think I deserve a break after the Alligator Farm." She glanced down at her torn hose.

"You go," said Hilda, "and I'll wait here with Mr. Hawthorn for the next trouble spot. Keep monitoring the news, Hawthorn."

"Yes, Madame," answered the miserable shopkeeper.

Sabrina tried to look casual as she strolled past the fortune-teller's shop, which was down a flight of stairs on the basement level. She paused, pretending to be looking at a tie-dyed dress in the shop window above. But she was really trying to see what was happening in the gypsy's salon. Blinds in the lower window, which had been open, suddenly dropped shut.

Making an executive decision, Sabrina motioned with a flick of her wrist to her dad across the street. He crossed the street casually, getting sympathetic looks from other smelly people dressed in rags. When he finally joined her, they both looked around to make sure nothing was wrong. With no monsters in sight, they ducked down the stairwell.

Edward rapped on the door, while Sabrina kept lookout on the street. She was beginning to feel like a spy in an old movie from the 1970s. Any moment, she expected a bunch of masked karate guys to jump out of the shrubs. She gripped the Witchopoly board tightly under her arm, hoping she could get rid of it soon.

When the door didn't open, Edward barked testily, "Come on, Madame Lavant! We know you're in there. Open up!"

"Please!" urged Sabrina.

With a fumbling of locks and bolts, the door finally opened a crack. Madame Lavant gazed at them and hissed, "Go away! I don't need the trouble."

"Well, you've got it." Edward muscled past her and into her salon. Sabrina slipped in behind him and quickly locked the door. With great relief, she placed the Witchopoly game on the table in the center of the room.

"We hate to act like this," said Edward, "but you're the only hope we've got." He held out the black bag and shook it. "We have payment, too—more than you bargained for."

"Those monsters are after you!" insisted the woman fearfully. "They were *here!* They questioned me."

"Did you tell them anything?" asked Sabrina.

"I told them I saw you run past." The woman shivered. "Oh, that big one was so ugly. And he ate all my food!"

"They believed you?" asked Edward.

"How do I know what monsters believe? Now show me what's in that bag. It had better be good."

The fortune-teller leaned forward as Dad set the bag on the table and opened it. At once, the cache of jewels caught the candlelight and glimmered enticingly. Madame Lavant gasped with appreciation. "Are they real?"

"Don't quibble with me, Madame!" snapped Edward. "You asked an exorbitant fee for your advice, and here it is! Now please tell us how we can *win* this Witchopoly game."

The woman sighed and looked at Sabrina. "Are you sure you weren't followed?"

"To tell you the truth, we aren't sure of anything," answered the teenager. "We're in a mess, and if you can do anything to help us, please do it."

Coming to a decision, Madame Lavant nodded and gazed at Edward. "You're stuck in a numerical loop, right? You can't use your powers or go home until you roll a certain number."

"Yes!" he answered eagerly. "One! I have to roll a *one.*"

"You are in luck." She leaned forward and

whispered, "The trick my brother always used on me was—"

"Yes? Yes?"

"Magical dice. He bought them in a magic store. They were supposed to roll a seven, although you could make them roll whatever number you wanted." She seethed with anger. "Oh, I hated him when I found out about those dice. No wonder he always won!"

"Would that work for us?" asked Sabrina doubtfully.

"It always worked for my rotten brother," snapped the fortune-teller. "And I still have the dice. Let me get them for you." Muttering to herself, the woman ducked into the doorway with the hanging beads,

Dad turned to Sabrina, but he didn't look very happy. "I was hoping for something better than magical dice. That could backfire on us."

Sabrina stood up and paced nervously. She saw movement outside the door, and she started to warn her dad. But the shadows vanished, except for pedestrians moving past on the sidewalk. Sabrina had to admit that she was feeling jumpy and scared—she just wanted to get this day over with.

"It's your decision, Dad."

The beads parted, and Madame Lavant shuffled back into the room. She gave them a large yawn, then set two identical six-sided dice on the table beside the Witchopoly die. "Do you see? They look exactly like the one with the game."

That had been enough to fool a little girl, thought Sabrina, *but will it be enough to fool the Witchopoly board itself?*

The fortune-teller slumped into her chair and yawned again. "Oh, I don't know why I'm so tired . . . all of the excitement, I guess."

Edward yawned, too, and picked up one of the magical die. "I think we should try it. What about you, Sabrina?"

The teenager woke up from a brief doze, still standing on her feet. She blinked with confusion at her dad. "What were you asking?"

"I don't remember." He looked at their hostess, but the fortune-teller was asleep, with her head resting on the table.

"How rude," said Sabrina.

In a foggy daze, Edward glanced around the room, and alarm slowly spread across his handsome face. "Oh, no!"

"What's the matter?"

Swaying back and forth, Edward rose to his feet. In his clumsiness, he dropped the die from his hand, and it rolled against the others. "It must be a sleep spell. Or sleeping gas in the air—"

Sabrina touched the walls, as if feeling their solidity would help her stay upright. Suddenly there were footsteps on the stairs outside, and a heavy hand yanked on the doorknob. When the intruder found the door locked, a hairy fist smashed through the window and fumbled with the knob.

"Dad!" screamed Sabrina. Another loud noise came from the back of the apartment, and she knew that someone had just tumbled down the coal chute.

Edward quickly gathered up the Witchopoly board and all three dice, not knowing which was which. "Get close to me!" he ordered.

"How close?"

"Like . . . turn real small, and jump into my pocket!"

With monsters attacking from both sides, Sabrina didn't even question her dad's request. She tried to clear her groggy mind and concentrate on a spell:

"Higgity piggity, fuss and bother,
I'll do anything to please my father.
So make me tiny—make me small.
Get me into his pocket before I fall!"

Just as the door smashed open and the ferocious yeti staggered into the room, Sabrina zipped through the air like a miniature rocket ship. She shot into the comforting darkness of her dad's pocket and waited for him to save them.

But what is he going to do? she suddenly realized. *Without any magic!*

Sabrina closed her eyes and waited for the monsters to crunch them.

☆

Chapter 11

☆

In the darkness of her dad's pocket, Sabrina was startled by the trumpet of an elephant. *Did Salem have elephants working for him now?* She couldn't see anything in her dad's pocket, which was like a large sleeping bag. Nobody had crunched them—so she tried to reverse the spell:

"Being small is fun, but it's not all.
I'm ready to go back to being tall!"

With a ripping sound, Sabrina grew to her normal size and tumbled out of her dad's pocket. To her horror, she found herself staring at the ground—about a hundred feet below her!

Looking around in a panic, Sabrina discovered that she and her dad were perched on a narrow metal platform high in the air. Below them were hundreds of cheering fans, plus a menagerie of elephants, lions, horses, dogs, and other animals.

"Don't make a move," cautioned a familiar voice. With steady hands, Dad grabbed her collar and lifted her carefully to her feet. Being afraid of heights, she gripped him like a life preserver.

"Where *are* we?" she squeaked.

"Circus World. On the tightrope platform."

"What?" Sabrina was even more horrified to look down and see that the only way off their lofty perch was a rope about an inch thick. It seemed to stretch forever into the distance before meeting up with the other platform. There was also a narrow ladder, but she could never look down long enough to climb on it.

Panicking, Sabrina looked up. She saw that they weren't far from the top pole of the mammoth tent. Knowing this, she was able to calm down and start breathing again. "You used the Luck card to get us here," she told her dad. "But how?"

"Remember, things don't work in the game like you think they will. The game gave me the power to go to Circus World. It didn't say there was a *time limit* on that power, so I could use it anytime." He gave her a grim smile. "I was hopeful it would work, but I wasn't sure."

"And the monsters?"

Hesitantly, Dad looked down at the ground . . . which was still too far away. Sabrina forced herself to look down, too, but she didn't see any yeti, harpies, or lizard men mixed in with the horses and elephants.

Of course, the stupid game couldn't deposit them safely in the stands. Oh, no. It had to put them on the highest perch in Circus World— with no safety net!

Fortunately, a chimpanzee show was occupying the crowd's attention in the left ring, and acrobats were juggling and tumbling in the right ring. From their vantage point, it appeared that a troupe of clowns was getting ready to take center ring—right beneath them.

"I don't see Salem and his crew," answered Dad with relief. "We almost lost it that last time. Before anything else happens, we've got to finish the game."

"Up here?" asked Sabrina.

"No one's looking at us, and no one can sneak up on us," answered Dad. He motioned to the rickety ladder. "Of course, we could always climb down."

"No, no! That's all right," Sabrina hastily assured him. "I could use magic to get us down."

"All I have to do is roll a one," answered Dad with a sly smile. "And I've got loaded dice."

"Are we going to cheat?"

Her dad sighed and held up three identical dice. "I don't think we have any choice. In all the commotion, I got the dice mixed up."

"Okay," muttered Sabrina, pointing to the Witchopoly board. "Lay it down. Before you get to roll, it's my turn."

After Dad set up the board, he held the three dice in the palm of his hand. Sabrina picked the closest one. That was something her mom had taught her—always pick the closest one.

Sabrina looked down at the board, trying not to look over the edge. She tried not to think how absurd it was that they were playing a board game on a tiny platform, hundreds of feet in the air.

"Anytime tonight," suggested her dad.

"Right." Sabrina was about to roll the die when a shrieking whistle came from below them. It was followed by a siren and enough honks for rush-hour traffic. She looked down and was momentarily blinded by spotlights. At once, Sabrina was in a panic, thinking they would be discovered, like in the disco.

A strong hand steadied her shoulder. "It's all right, Sweetheart. It's just the clowns."

Sabrina opened her eyes to see that the lights were trained on the center ring, not them. The ring was full of clowns, racing around in little cars and wagons. With huge hammers, squirt bottles, and buckets of confetti, other clowns were trying to fix the runaway cars. It was bedlam, with one car disgorging at least ten clowns.

The delighted laughter of children echoed all the way up to the platform, and Sabrina relaxed a bit. She couldn't help but smile at the wild antics of the clowns, who were very funny and acrobatic. In this cheerful place, it didn't seem possible for anything bad to happen to them.

Suddenly many of the clowns were flying through the air, as if propelled by cannons. Sabrina was amazed at these stunts—it looked more like TV wrestling than a clown act. She saw other clowns running away, leaping out of the center ring and not coming back. That didn't seem very funny, and even the audience muttered and booed.

Sabrina was a long way from the action, and it was hard to find the cause of the commotion. Finally she saw *them*—a carload of hideous monsters dressed like clowns. With slithery tentacles and barbed claws, they scrambled from a hole in the ground and rampaged across the center ring. They drove the real clowns from the spotlight with their own oversized hammers and squirters.

Some of the audience laughed at this turn of

events, but Sabrina wasn't laughing. A ringmaster strode into the ring, carrying a microphone. He was dressed in a bright red tuxedo, but black fur bulged from the gaps of his tight jacket. Audience members screamed at this addition to the cast, and some of them dashed for the exits. But others waited to see whether this monstermaster was part of the show.

We're about to become part of the show, feared Sabrina.

"Roll the dice!" urged her father. "Take your turn."

"Which dice! This one!" She held up the die she had selected, not knowing whether it was a magic one or not. With a worried cringe, Sabrina tossed the die—it came up four.

"Four!" exclaimed her dad puzzledly. "Why did you roll that? You landed on a blank space."

Sabrina laughed apologetically. "I forgot to think of which number I should roll. So I just threw it."

A loud drumroll sounded, almost jarring them out of their lofty perch. Both of them leaned over to see the ringmaster strutting about, while his clowns capered in the audience. They stole womens' hats and babies' candy, and the audience wasn't sure whether to laugh or run away.

The ringmaster whistled loudly, and his monstrous crew stopped their antics and scampered back into the ring. He addressed the crowd, and Salem's familiar voice droned over the loudspeaker:

"Ladies and gentlemen, trolls and ghouls! For your edification and enlightenment, we offer the most death-defying act on the midway. Look upward, high into the tent poles of the big top. See them risk their lives for you—the tightrope walkers!"

Now blazing lights struck Sabrina and Edward, forcing them to duck out of sight. But there wasn't any place to hide on the small, swaying platform. Sabrina tried to stand up, but she couldn't see with the lights glaring in her eyes. She finally sat back down, trying to think of what she could do to save them.

Dad used his hand to shield his eyes. "They're still far away from us. I'm going to finish this game." He grabbed one of the die and started to roll, when the sound of flapping wings surrounded them.

A harpy soared into the light and sprang upon her father, sinking claws into his back and slashing at his head. Sabrina jumped up, balling her hands into fists, when a thing that looked like a winged goat on steroids suddenly swooped from the darkness. She threw a punch, but the beast kicked with his hooves and forced her to her knees.

On the shaky platform, Sabrina and Edward

fought for their lives against these winged nightmares from old Greece. The monsters bit and kicked, trying to push them off the platform into the sawdust far below. The flying creatures had no fear, because *they* weren't going to fall.

Her dad groaned under the relentless attack of the shrieking harpy. Sabrina felt the ladder shake as other monsters climbed up from below. There was no escape—they were cut off! She tried to cast a spell, but she couldn't concentrate while a flying goat was kicking her in the face.

In desperation, Dad threw the only thing in his hand—the die—at the screeching harpy. It exploded in the monster's face like a fireball, sending him spiraling into the darkness. At once, the Witchopoly board began to glow and hum like a live-wire, and Sabrina realized that her dad had thrown the magic die.

The goat and the other flying monsters had the good sense to escape, fluttering quickly in reverse. Dad tried to touch the board, but it sizzled like acid, burning his fingers.

"Ow!" he howled. "Let's get out of here! It's gonna blow!" He grabbed her hand and pulled her in the only direction available—across the tightrope.

"Dad!" screamed the teen with alarm. "I'm not going out there!" Suddenly the Witchopoly board began to pop and sparkle, as if a hundred tiny firecrackers were embedded inside it. Sabrina gulped, kicked off her shoes, and scurried after her dad onto the thick rope. The audience cheered wildly, thinking this was the high point of the show.

"There's nothing to it," insisted Dad nervously. "Just keep the rope on the balls of your feet—the fat part."

"My feet are not fat," claimed Sabrina. She took a step forward . . . and instantly slipped off. She fell with one leg on each side of the rope, which caught her in the stomach and made her spin around. She managed to catch the rope and hold on with both hands as her legs dropped away into nothingness.

"Help!" she squeaked in panic.

Her dad was swaying back and forth on the rope, waving his arms and trying to keep his balance. "Whoa! Whoa! Look out!"

Edward finally pitched forward and managed to catch the rope under his armpits. He hung there, swaying in the opposite direction from her, and it felt as if they were holding on to a snake.

"Well, it can't get any worse than this!" muttered Dad, panting for breath.

A huge explosion of magical might ripped the tightrope platform, eliciting cries from the crowd. Sizzling sparks rained down on Sabrina and her dad, as the rope broke from the flaming platform and swung free.

Sabrina and Edward were in a good position to hang on, but they screamed in terror as they fell hundreds of feet, hanging on to the rope. Still screaming, they swooped over the heads of the monsters, who leaped and lunged at them.

But the rope held taut and swung them upward toward the audience, who applauded with delight. As they sailed over the bleachers, Sabrina screamed, "I can't hold on!"

"Let go!" answered Dad.

At the end of the upswing, they let go of the rope and glided over the heads of the startled audience. Sabrina closed her eyes, expecting to crash into a tent pole or a monster. She was pleasantly surprised when her momentum propelled her into something soft and sticky.

She shook her head and opened her eyes—and found herself sprawled in a haystack. A hand brushed her hair, and she reached up to grab the hand and ask, "Are you all right?"

The appendage felt uncomfortably like a python, and Sabrina yanked her hand back and screamed. Nevertheless, the elephant snorted, lowered his trunk, and persisted in eating his hay.

Behind her, a clump of hay moved, and her dad poked his head out. "Are we alive?"

"I think so. But I don't think the Witchopoly game survived."

Edward rubbed his eyes and looked glum. "I may never get my powers back now. Will you still love me when I'm a regular mortal? When I'm old and gray?"

"Sure, Dad," answered Sabrina with a winning smile. "I loved you long before I knew about witches and warlocks."

Suddenly, they heard scuffling sounds behind them, and they both tried to burrow deeper into the hay. Finally it was Dad who shook his head and sat up. "I'm tired of running away. Let's see who it is."

They stumbled out of the haystack in time to see six burly guys rush down the aisle and tackle the ringmaster. They dragged Salem to the ground in the center ring, while the audience applauded happily. The monsters started to attack the rescue crew, but they drove them into the shadows with fireballs and magical bolts.

"Best show I've ever seen at Circus World!" gushed a lady in the audience.

"Let me up!" growled Salem, struggling under the burly men. "Let me up, or I'll turn you all into toads!"

From another aisle, Aunt Hilda strode into the circus ring and pointed her finger ominously at Salem. "You'll knock it off, or there will be no more tuna fish. Not even on your *birthday!*"

The horrid beast cringed at that threat, and Sabrina could see a glimmer of Salem in him. She wanted to rush forward and hug her aunt, but it was clear that Hilda was on a roll. Glaring at the black monster, the witch raised her arms and said:

"I hearby invoke a certain decree
That the Witchcs' Council settled on thee.
A cat you were; a cat you will be.
I end the curse of Witchopoly!"

The ringmaster uniform exploded with a puff of smoke. When the smoke cleared, there was no more big, black monster—just a frightened, little kitty.

Sabrina ran forward to hug her aunt, and her dad was right behind her. "Sabrina!" said Hilda with shocked amazement. "Edward! We saw the game explode, and we thought we were too late."

"Is that the Bomb Squad?" asked Edward with relief.

"Yes, and they say they can turn everything back to normal."

"Normal," repeated Edward, sounding as if he couldn't imagine such a thing existed. The audience was still on their feet, applauding madly, so Edward turned to give them a gracious bow.

Finally Sabrina walked over to pick up a trembling black cat. She scolded him. "Salem, you've been a bad kitty."

"I know," he muttered sheepishly. "But it was so much fun."

The party continued on the patio of Edward's villa. It was night, and the sea was now dark—but they could hear the whisper of waves splashing against the shore. Aunt Hilda was there, and so were Byron and Mr. Hawthorn, both of whom were extremely relieved.

Mr. Hawthorn had furnished all the refreshments, and he never stopped apologizing to everyone in sight. He was so happy that no bad publicity had gotten out about the Winsome Witch. Byron kept flirting with her, but Sabrina kept her mind on Harvey. Once before, she had made the mistake of liking a warlock too much.

Byron admitted that he had met Harvey, and he told her it was cool that she was so loyal . . . to a mortal. Sabrina decided that she might shop at the Winsome Witch a little more often.

She called Harvey and told him that she would make it up to him for deserting him today. But after all, it was Father's Day. Curiously, he couldn't remember how he had spent the day at all.

Gail was coming over, just as soon as she finished with the Witches' Council. But they couldn't get Aunt Zelda to leave the Disco Dimension. The Bomb Squad had fixed things and gone back to their thicket, which couldn't be as big as Aunt Hilda described it.

Sabrina sipped her chocolate milk shake and listened to Hilda talk about how she had saved the day. Well, she had been awfully smart to listen to the news and round up the Bomb Squad. But to Sabrina, it had still been her dad who had saved the day. She couldn't believe how dashing and daring he had been, even without his powers.

Dad sat beside her, smiling at her from time to time. After their wild adventure, they were inseparable, afraid to leave each other's side. They needn't have worried, because all the monsters had been captured and returned to the Dark Woods. Salem was at home, locked in the bathroom.

"I'm sorry, Dad," she whispered. "You deserved a better Father's Day than this."

"Are you kidding? It was the best Father's Day I ever had! Want to see me do some magic?"

"It's okay, Dad," she said with a smile. "I'm glad you got your magic back. I just wanted to get you a really cool gift, so I would have an excuse to come by and hang with you. I'm sorry it backfired."

He put his arm around her shoulders. "You don't need any excuse at all, Princess. You can come by for a visit whenever you feel like it. I think we proved today that we can have fun, even under the worst of circumstance. Just do me one favor."

"Yes?"

"Next time, ditch the cat."

About the Author

John Vornholt has done many things in his life, from being a factory worker to being a stuntman, but writing has always been his first love. He's written for magazines, television, movies, the theater, and computer companies, and he really enjoys writing books and telling a story one reader at a time.

John lives with his wife, two kids, and two dogs in Arizona. Check out his Web page at http://www.sff.net/people/vornholt.

American SISTERS

Join different sets of sisters
as they embark on the varied,
sometimes dangerous,
always exciting journeys
that crossed America's landscape!

West Along the Wagon Road, 1852

A Titanic Journey Across the Sea, 1912

Voyage to a Free Land, 1630

Adventure on the Wilderness Road, 1775

By Laurie Lawlor

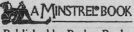 A MINSTREL BOOK
Published by Pocket Books   2106